THIRD GIRL
FROM THE LEFT

by
Ann Turner

Macmillan Publishing Company
New York

To Jane,
who first said, "I like it,"
and to Judy,
for her trust

Macmillan Publishing Company
866 Third Avenue, New York, NY 10022
Collier Macmillan Canada, Inc.
Printed in the United States of America
10 9 8 7 6 5 4 3 2 1
The text of this book is set in 12 pt. Electra.
Library of Congress Cataloging-in-Publication Data
Turner, Ann Warren.
Third girl from the left.
Summary: Itching to do something different, eighteen-
year-old Sarah leaves Maine for the harsh Montana
environment as a mail-order bride, and is soon left a
widow with a 2000-acre ranch to run.
[1. Ranch life—Montana—Fiction.   2. Montana—Fiction.]   1. Title.
PZ7.T8535Th   1986   [Fic]   85-30028
ISBN 0-02-789510-6

CHAPTER ONE

"First," Goody ticked off on one blunt finger, "there was the day you put molasses on the minister's saddle."

Sarah smiled at the memory. Mr. Rowner's mouth had become a goose's egg as he tried to rise in his saddle and could not. "Oh—oh—oh," he puffed, struggling to free himself.

"He deserved it, Aunt!" she said decisively. "If he hadn't been so infernally boring, I wouldn't have done it. Everyone slept through his sermons; Pa snored louder than anyone else. I can't bear being bored, Goody, you know that."

Goody raised an eyebrow and went on. "*Then*, there was the time you put a pinch of gunpowder in the school stove— lucky it only made a small bang. . . . The trouble with you is, you don't think, you just *do*."

Well, I did choose carefully, Sarah thought. She hadn't wanted to harm anyone, just shake them up. That prim-faced schoolmarm, buttons up to her double chin, spouting salvation day in and day out. Besides, the teacher had rapped Sarah's knuckles almost daily for talking. I couldn't help it, Sarah thought. My mouth just wants to talk.

" 'Course, I won't even go into the time you and Cissy stole the clothes from the men's swimming hole and Charlie Blackmun had to crawl home stark naked through the blueberry bushes and bring back blankets. That ruined several proposals, Niece."

"Yes, Aunt," Sarah said demurely, knowing Goody was

1

not fooled. She opened the oven door with the top of her boot to let more heat into the farm kitchen. Cold for the third week of March, Sarah thought, with a heavy snow just yesterday. It seemed spring would never come. She wondered if Pa was still in the barn, feeding the cows.

Goody ticked off the last finger of her left hand. She held it up and shook it vehemently. "Do you see this, Sary? One whole hand full of foolish, sinful pranks!"

"What were the other two, Aunt?" Sarah asked, her foot tapping the stove hob.

Goody looked exasperated, two gray curls springing out from her cheeks. "Only two years ago—and you a woman of sixteen—you drew Mr. Abram's name from the church grab bag to make a Christmas present for. And what did you do?"

Sarah chuckled and thought she saw Goody's lips twitch.

"You knit him a nose warmer—a nose warmer with two ties to go around his head—in pink, too!" Goody began to laugh, sputters changing to loud hoots.

"You wick-ed girl—it took him *months* to get over it! Every time someone came into his store they'd ask, 'How's your nose, Frank? Keeping warm, eyuh?' "

"The fifth, Aunt, what was the fifth?" Beans, the tomcat, rubbed against her skirts and arched his back as sleet hissed against the black window.

"Oh, that was quite a prank, Niece. When the minister's wife got in the family way, an event that took five years, you snuck into church and chalked up a different opening hymn: 'God Moves in A Mysterious Way.' I never saw a man blush such a peculiar color before, sort of—"

"Like canned tomatoes, Aunt."

"Mmm, or crushed raspberries." Goody took up her knit-

2

ting and the needles clicked ominously. "If your ma had lived, maybe you wouldn't be so wild. Your pa ain't exactly convivial, as the ladies' journals say, and you lived alone with him for two years before I came. I think that's what did it," she said, more to herself than to Sarah. "Those two ungoverned years."

Sarah did not answer. She didn't know if those two lonely years had made her wild. Angry, yes; sad, yes; but wild?

"Well, what do y'plan on doing, Sary?"

"About what, Aunt?"

"Gettin' married! Is there anything else to plan on in this life?" she snapped. "Do you want to be the only girl of your age who's not married?"

"But, Aunt, you didn't marry and you've had a good life."

"Have I, Sary? Always an aunt, never a mother?" Goody looked down her broad nose. "Besides, here you are, eighteen years old and no one—not *one* suitor! Alan Beals was interested. . . ."

"Goody! You know I can't bear his ma!"

"Well, she is a little—"

"Eats, breathes, and *sleeps* the Bible, Goody. We'd have to live with her and I'd strangle her in a day."

"Hold your tongue, Niece! She's a good woman, full of good works."

"Knitting dusters for Africans," Sarah muttered.

"And what's wrong with that?" Goody inquired. "It's *exactly* huts as needs dusting, my girl. Now, what about Jimmy Carpenter? He's got a good farm—apple orchards, fifty acres in pasture, two woodlots. He was interested for a while, 'least until that time you stole the men's clothes from the swimming hole and—"

3

Sarah broke in, "Dull as mud, Goody. He can hardly talk, and when he does, it's cows and dung, teats and hay, milk and his dear sainted mother. . . ."

"Child! That's what I mean! You'll never get a husband if you talk that way. Scares 'em off." She sighed. "Men are easily frightened, Niece."

Sarah glanced at her: That was Goody's story as well. When she was sixteen, she was engaged to a young suitor with prospects at sea. He left on a two-year voyage, waving good-bye to a reasonable-sized girl. When he returned, Goody was six feet tall, with hands and feet like Paul Bunyan's.

Sarah patted her aunt's knee. "I know, Goody—I do try, but no one here suits me. And I just can't seem to get this courtship thing right. When we go for walks, they stop to pick daisies and I stride ahead. When they pick apple blossoms, I'm figuring out how many bushels of apples that tree'll give. I want to *run* a farm, not be somebody's drudge, all worn out at thirty with no teeth left."

They sat for a moment, looking at the stove and not at each other.

Sarah stopped rocking. "Tell me, Goody, how many women do we know who've died before forty?"

Goody made a *tcch*ing sound.

Sarah ticked off on her fingers, "One: Lucy Warren— six children in eight years, a husband who kept saying, 'I thought I married a *good worker!*' wore out at thirty-eight and died."

Goody shifted in her chair.

"Two: Sally Tippet—four children in four years, and a husband who refused to hire a girl to help her with the work. Died of an unknown complaint at thirty." Sarah stood up and

4

chanted. "Wash on Monday, iron on Tuesday, bake on Wednesday, churn on Thursday, sew and mend on Friday, do all the dairy work, the chicken and cows, *plus* tend to the little dears' education, and what do you have?"

She sat down and thumped the chair arm. "A worn-out drudge—that's what!"

Goody was silent for a time. "Well, it is true that some women just have too much work, Sary. But what would you rather be? A spinster? A teacher living like a hired girl in someone else's house?"

"I don't know." Sarah stuck her tongue between her teeth.

"Really, Niece." Goody rocked faster. "You've no sense at all—no sense! The only good thing about you is your size. Men do like small women."

"With small voices," Sarah whispered.

"And small hands and feet." Goody sighed.

And small minds, Sarah wanted to add. Why can't I be like other girls? she wondered. Did she want too much? Just today, it had been brought home to her again how different she was, like a white cow in a herd of brown. She'd been at the ladies' sewing circle (Wednesday, Mrs. Black's house), and had knocked on the gray, weather-stained door.

"Come in, come in!" Abigail Pierce held the door open. A drift of snow blew off the roof, down Sarah's neck.

"Ooh, cold!" She leaped inside, shook herself like a dog, and handed her worn cloak to Abigail, who smiled uncertainly, as if Sarah were a foreign dish too spicy to eat.

Sarah went into the parlor and stood by the potbellied stove. In the corner, two children played silently, tugging the arms of a rag doll in opposite directions. Cissy raised her head

5

and smiled at Sarah, needle flashing in and out of the skirt in her lap. Anna Hew kept talking to Emily Merrit, a woman with a sunken chest and one row of teeth.

"And then, of course, there she was—four months gone with five children already, and worn out like a rag. She just couldn't carry it!"

"Tch!" Emily Merrit sucked her teeth.

"She shouldn't have married Ted Brown, then," said Mrs. Black, a mountainous woman with a bosom like a laundry basket. "A man like that—a child every year." She shook her head.

"Tch!" The room rustled with disapproval. Sarah wasn't sure if it was disapproval of Ted Brown and his selfish desires or of Mrs. Black, who tended to be "coarse," as Cissy said. Besides, the married women weren't supposed to talk of such matters before the unwed ones—Cissy and Sarah.

Sarah sat next to her friend and took out her crochet hook and thread. "Anything new?" she whispered.

" 'Course not, 'cept Emily's cousin ran away to get married," Cissy said.

"Did she now?" Sarah smiled. That showed spirit, someone with enough gumption to escape this suffocating town. "Is that all that happened?"

"No." Cissy smiled. "I'm engaged to Dan Monroe. He asked me last night."

"Engaged? Cissy! You told me he was like kissing a horse. *You* said . . ."

Cissy shushed her. "That was before. He asked, I mean. He's a nice boy," she whispered more loudly, "and besides, Sarah, I don't want to live with Ma and Pa the rest of my life."

6

Sarah did not look at her. Second best—or third, that's what Dan was. Was that what life was, always taking the next-best thing? Calamity Jane wouldn't marry a man who kissed like a horse. Sarah was sure of it. She'd been reading about her in *Beadle's Pocket Library*—a true wild woman of the West. What she wanted, she did!

"Say you're happy for me," Cissy nudged her.

Sarah did not smile. She felt frightened and alone, the only girl now of their class at school who had not married, except for Annie Belton, and she had a hump, so that didn't count.

"Say you're happy," her friend insisted.

"I'm happy," Sarah mumbled.

The talk surged around them, Mrs. Black's voice the loudest. "Johnny's teeth are coming in, and he's up all night, crying. Seems like I hardly get a chance to sleep nowadays."

"Ah, yes." Murmurs of sympathy came from the other mothers. "I remember my Alice—my Bob—cried for days, weeks—terrible."

On and on, Sarah thought. Marriages and teeth, babies and miscarriages, the mystery of couples who had children and those who didn't, fleas and piles, the treatment for ague, footrot in cows, husbands who were surly, houses that grew dust, and always health—like some precarious bridge that could sway and splinter under you at any moment.

She felt itchy under her collar and yanked the thread over the hook, pulling in and out, over and under. Even Cissy was intent on her work, needle stitching cloth. Sarah stared outside at the rain. She stared at the worn spot in the dark brown rug and tapped her foot. The talk went on.

7

"And then Mrs. Potter told me Dan's going to put the high acreage into corn this June."

The two children shrieked in the corner, arguing over a doll, and Mrs. Black turned around and shushed them.

"Corn!"

"She might have enough for a parlor organ if it does well."

"Organ! We could have hymn sings. . . ."

Sarah's feet tapped more quickly. They were small and shapely, her one vanity. And her arms were strong and wiry under the blue wool dress, arms made for something besides sewing circles and chitchat.

The snow drifted past the window and the fire settled in the stove. Emily coughed hoarsely. Sarah wondered what would happen if she screamed.

"Frank's having trouble with his teeth."

"Eyuh, so's Reuben. 'Course his Uncle Bob just passed away. We'll have to go all the way to Portland for the funeral."

"Portland!"

Suddenly, Sarah could bear it no more. They would drag her down with their talk of teeth and death, when she was like a horse at the starting line, glossy, rounded, ready to race.

She rose quickly, tumbling her lace into the workbag. "Abigail? Sorry to leave so soon—work at home." She pushed her way through the sewing circle, ignoring Cissy's look of surprise. Grabbing her cloak, Sarah rushed outside into the biting wind and snow, down the road, past the maple blasted by lightning, past the pond where the men swam—never the women—to the snowy fields of home.

She stood at the top of the rise and looked down at Pa's farm. Gray house, small and crooked as the proverbial shoe.

8

Orchard of used-up trees. Gray barn with twenty cows drooling and blowing inside. Things went in one end and came out the other, day after day, year after year, until you went crazy with the sameness of it, like Hannah Turner, who took a train to the sea and walked in, hat and all, never looking back.

"I try, Aunt, I really do!" she burst out, scaring the cat and Goody into wakefulness. "I try to be like other girls, but it never works—it won't *ever* work!"

"Then what's to do?" Goody murmured sleepily.

"I don't know, Goody." Sarah rocked faster. "But I'll find something, you'll see. I'm not going to stay in Dewborne, Maine, the rest of my days, watching my teeth fall out and walking over to cemetery hill to look at my plot! I'm going to *do* something so they can carve words on that stone besides SARAH BLANK-BLANK, 10 CHILDREN, DEARLY BELOVED DRUDGE, GONE HOME."

CHAPTER TWO

Sarah settled the chickens for the night, securing the fence against foxes. It was a never-ending battle between teeth and knife; sometimes the fox's teeth got the hens first, other times her knife won. She went into the barn and patted Sam's nose, rubbing the soft velvet. Then she ran her hand along the horse's fat, furred side.

Maybe this is the only warmth you'll ever get, Sarah Goodhue, a nasty voice said inside her. *Old horses and chickens for warmth—how sad.*

Sarah pulled the shawl over her head. Sleet wet her face as she strode across the frozen barnyard to the kitchen steps. Through the window, she saw Pa sitting in his rocking chair— breathing and rocking, breathing and rocking. His fringe of gray hair blew out as he rocked, and his long face was pale in the lamplight. Her hands twisted inside the shawl. She might live here forever—gray house closing in on her like a coffin, watching Pa and Goody age and wither, watching other girls marry—even fools. She sucked in her breath, suddenly afraid. What choices did she have? She'd thought about working in the mills in Biddeford, or as far away as Manchester. Just for the change. But what news she'd had about the mills made them sound worse than Dewborne. Stuffy buildings with the machinery rickety-clacketing all day long. Landladies who insisted on church and served watery soup. And hours longer

10

than the hours on a farm. That was no change. Goody's words kept plucking at her like a worrisome child: But what would you rather be?"

Sarah stamped her foot. Marry—or not. Work yourself to death in a mill—or not. Someone—was it God?—had planned things very badly where women were concerned. She slammed into the kitchen and flung her shawl on a chair.

Pa leaped out of his chair. "Eh—Sary? Can't you ever be quiet?" He stared at her as she bustled about the kitchen, closing cupboard doors, stacking the supper dishes, and putting them away. She grabbed the Portland paper and sat in the rocking chair opposite his.

"Goody gone up to bed?" she asked, without looking up.

"Eyuh, she was tired." Warily, Pa sat down again and scratched his nose. Sarah looked like a cat that had been fuzzed the wrong way; brown hair frizzing around her face, fingers prickling on the page, even her mouth looked electrified.

Sarah opened the newspaper. "Traveler writes of riding the railroad West," she read silently. "Across the prairie, past antelope and game and inspiring mountains, all the way to the coast." What she wouldn't give to ride that railroad, clickety-clacking to someplace new and fresh!

"There's a story here about going West, Pa."

"Mmm." He rocked and pulled on his left ear.

"It'd be something to see real Indians, wouldn't it?" She thought of them riding their swift, small ponies, black hair blowing in the wind.

Pa grunted.

Sarah glared at him. It was like trying to have a conversation with a cow! She turned the page, rustling it just for the

11

noise. Suddenly, Sarah stopped rocking and planted her feet on the floor. The hair seemed to settle and smooth around her face.

"Pa?" She slapped the paper. "There's an ad here, for a bride out in Montana Territory."

"Bride?" Pa repeated stupidly. "Montana?"

"Listen!" She read in a high, excited voice, "Wanted, a wife of docile temper to care for husband and hands. Ranch in high country with one thousand head of cattle. Wife must be able to cook, sew, read, and, God willing, talk. Direct all replies to Alex T. Proud, High Ridge Ranch, Dillman, Montana."

"A ranch," she mused. "That would give a body some scope. You wouldn't feel all closed in on a ranch." Maybe she'd meet Calamity Jane there—meet someone who'd chosen a different life, not houses, children, drudgery, or the mill, but a romantic life outside under the stars. Free.

"Ha!" Pa snorted. "Docile temper?"

Sarah chuckled.

"Talk—you can do that, Sary! Your mouth is like the barn door, always flapping open and shut. Only what comes out ain't pigs and chickens. Can you ride talk? No! Can you eat it? No! Then, Lord, what good is it?"

Sarah stared at him. "That's the longest speech you've ever given, Pa."

"Well." He subsided in his chair. "Well."

Maybe that was why Ma had died early, Sarah thought, slipping away like some child ghost in her long nightgown, searching for talk. Could Montana be any worse than this? Sleet against the window, wind hustling under her skirt, and dead silence forever and ever?

12

"Well," she said impatiently, "what do you think?"

"About what?" Pa rocked back and forth.

"About me being a bride!" The cat skittered behind the stove. "About going on the railroad out West. About me marrying, Pa." Ever after, she wondered if she would have chosen to go if Pa hadn't driven her wild with his mutters and rocking.

He opened his gray eyes and looked directly at her. "What I think don't matter, Sary. You'll please yourself, just as you always do." He closed his eyes and commenced rocking.

Sarah almost spat. She wasn't going to stay here and live like him: one wife, dead ten years; one child; and one trip to Portland in fifty years. That was no life, poured out like some skinny blue milk, a dribble here, a dribble there, until you died in your rocking chair dreaming of food.

Sarah threw the paper on the floor, went to the wall cupboard, and took down Ma's book on the American West. She thumbed through it to the center, touching the worn page edges. The book flopped open to an etching of tall, sharp mountains rising straight up from a plain. She sighed. It was always the same, seeing this, like a drink of cool water.

Ma had loved mountains. Maybe the mountains on High Ridge looked like these, Sarah thought, and whenever she looked out the window, her heart would rise up. Maybe second best would feel like first best out in new, wild country. I'll go, she thought; why not? She arranged it neatly in her mind. Goody would stay with Pa—he'd hardly miss her anyway. She felt the same excitement she had when putting the gunpowder into the school stove or the molasses on the minister's saddle. What a way to get out of this town! It had drama—dash—style. Besides, if she thought too much about it, she might lose her nerve.

13

She grabbed the inkwell, Ma's horn pen, a sheet of paper, and dashed off: "Dear Sir, I read your advertisement for a wife in the Portland paper and am interested. I've a mind to come West and marry, especially to someone who wants to talk. The *right* sort of talk is in short supply in Dewborne, Maine. I can do good plain cooking, sew, weave, doctor some, and handle horses. Father says I am gentle with cattle."

There. She wasn't exactly lying about a docile temper, but it was true about being gentle with animals.

"I am eighteen years of age, in good health, and never been wed. I like to sing."

Sarah lifted the pen. The advertisement had said nothing about pretty, so she didn't have to lie, although "pretty eyes" would not be stretching the truth.

"I am sending a daguerreotype taken last summer at the Fourth of July picnic. I am the third girl from the left, first row, in the bonnet with strawberries on top." Sarah knew the hat shaded her face—shaded her plainness.

"Would you please send a daguerreotype of yourself? Not that looks are important, but if you decide I'll suit, then I'll know who to look for at the station. If there is a station. If I don't suit, please return my picture.

"I await your reply, Sarah Adams Goodhue."

She rubbed her eyes and sighed, wondering what Goody would say when she found out. She hoped the letter was proper—not too forward but showing an interest. That was the problem, Sarah had decided some years ago; you never knew what to do when the *really* important things came along. Such as how to answer an ad for a bride. What to say to a bridegroom you'd never met. She shivered as she blotted the letter carefully with a clean scrap of flannel, then folded and slipped it into an envelope. "Mr. Alex T. Proud, High Ridge Ranch, Dillman, Montana," she penned on the outside, savoring the words. High Ridge—mountains—it would be all right.

"But Sarah . . ." Aunt Goody stood on the kitchen porch, meltwater dripping onto her bonnet. Her mouth was thin as spring ice. "I still don't understand. Why go so far away? Why so sudden? I thought you didn't want to get married."

Sarah grinned, waving the letter from Montana. "Why not, Aunt?" She rushed inside and slit open the letter. *This* would vindicate her, after two weeks of Goody's anxious, nagging questions. The answer had finally come.

She unfolded the crackling paper, and a daguerreotype and a smaller envelope fell on the kitchen table. Sarah seized the picture and held it up to the light. Better than she had dreamed—here was someone to show all. Here was a man— not some fat, overstuffed boy; not some dolt who talked only about his mother; not some ham-fisted, red-faced farmboy with chicken feathers behind his ears.

Two blunt fingers took the picture. "This is most peculiar, Niece. Look, the edges are worn and faded—why?"

Sarah grabbed the picture and held it to her chest. "Why do you make it so hard, Goody?" She turned over the picture. "He says on the back that it's a few years old, but it's all he has."

She looked at it again. Even in the stiff pose, she saw a lithe man astride a horse, hands firm on the reins. He had a full head of hair, a lean face with a moustache, and he was smiling.

"Well," Goody admitted grudgingly, "he is a handsome

15

man, Sary. Here, what does he say?" She took off her bonnet and sat down.

Together they read his reply.

Dear Miss Sarah Adams Goodhue,

   I was glad to receive your reply to my advertisement for a wife. I received a number of answers but yours seemed best to me, frank and straightforward. I shall be as frank.

   High Ridge Ranch is a fine one, though small, with one thousand head of cattle, a big house, and a separate cabin for the men. They handle all ranch work, and herd the beeves to the depot to be shipped East. It seems you Easterners can't get enough of our Western beef!

   I am enclosing a daguerreotype of myself taken a few years ago, when my first wife was alive. She died a year back. Women, especially *ladies*, are in short supply out here. That is why I advertised for a bride. I hope this letter answers any questions you may have. It won't be an easy life, Miss Goodhue, but I can promise you an interesting and worthwhile one in settling this beautiful new territory. A woman's influence is worth more than gold here, for you keep us civilized. I don't want to rush you, but it would be best to start without delay the long trip out here. It has been a long, cold winter. The journey is five days by rail and more than a day by stage to Dillman, and that's when the weather is good. Money for your journey is enclosed, and I will meet you at the Hotel Comfort in town whenever you say. We can be married there.

   If your father or guardian has any questions, please address them to me.

      Regards,
      Alex T. Proud

Goody snorted. "Talks a good deal, don't he? Still, he

16

does have a good head of hair and seems to have all of his teeth. Nothing I hate so much as a man with a sunken mouth. They suck and mumble so. Now, if he's all he says he is, Sary, you're very lucky. I wonder how old he is. Looks to be in his forties by the picture."

"He doesn't say, Aunt. But I expect anyone who runs his own ranch has to be pretty young and spry. He doesn't say anything about children, so he must be young." Sarah read the letter through a second time, imagining what the ranch would be like: land, acres and acres of it; prairie and mountains! She could ride a horse all day and not come to the end of it.

She looked inside the second, smaller envelope. "Seventy-five dollars, Goody!" She fingered the crisp, new money. "He must be a generous man."

"Mmmph." Goody peered over Sary's shoulder. "Alex T. Proud is an odd name. I hope he's not as odd as his name."

"Thank you for your encouragement, Aunt," Sarah said dryly, and folded the letter into its envelope.

"Oh, Sary." Goody touched her shoulder. "It's so sudden—we know so little of him—what if he . . . ?" She stopped and chewed on her thumb.

"If what, Goody?" Sarah stamped her foot. "You think I won't take a chance staying here and marrying Alan Beals or Jimmy Carpenter—assuming they'd still have me? Everything's a chance. Getting up in the morning, driving horses, breathing the night air—but I won't, I *won't* lie down and be buried alive in this village, Goody!"

"But . . ."

"No buts. I need a bigger place, Aunt. Living here is like—like wearing a too-tight corset all my days. But there"—

17

Sarah waved her arm—"there's mountains and clouds and wide spaces."

"There're clouds here, Sary," Goody said, and then hugged her. "All right, go—don't do as I did—sixty years old, never married, two day dresses, and living with a brother who talks less than the chickens. My day is done. A comfortable bed and a good fire are the sum of my wants."

Sarah squeezed her aunt's shoulders, feeling the resistance in them like sharp rocks that have withstood rain, flood, and storm. She wanted to say, *That's not enough, Aunt. You deserved more.* But she did not dare. Her head jerked up as the front door slammed.

Pa stomped into the kitchen, shedding wet as he came. He slung his coat over a chair and sat down. "Well, Sister, what do y' think of Sary's plans?" He nodded when Sarah gave him a cup of tea, white with milk and thick with four sugars.

Goody pushed at her hair. "I think it's a good idea, Frank. Sary's lived in Dewborne all her life, and I don't think that's enough for a girl of her—ah—temperament. A change'd do her good." She slapped her hands on her knees. "Oh, fuss, let's be honest. Sary'll *never* get a husband in Dewborne. You know it, Sary knows it, and I know it. We're not rich, she ain't good-lookin', and she's wild and undisciplined." Goody's smile softened her words. "Sary knows—she knows she's got to go, 'less she wants to stay on this farm and dry up like an old rooster."

"Well." Pa sniffed, slurped his tea, and sighed. "Maybe you're right. But Montana's more'n a change, Sister! I guess the young 'uns make their own way, and we have to take what's left, eh?"

18

Sarah clenched the letter. For the first time she felt sad—and guilty—about leaving. There was still time to back out if she wanted. The image of Goody and Pa left like washed-up bones on a beach made her chest ache. But then she thought of the straight figure on a Western horse, and the ache spread and disappeared like meltwater into the ground.

CHAPTER THREE

I'm nobody special, Sarah thought, as she packed and tied a crate of linens. Anyone could do what she was doing—anyone who was dying of suffocation, that is. But you'd think, the way people had carried on this last week, that she was going to Africa or China.

Cissy had run over almost every day on makeshift errands. "Here's a sewing kit for you, Sary." She held out a small, blue felt pocket embroidered with pink daisies. "Think of me when you sew."

"Oh, Cissy. You're not going sentimental on me, are you?"

Cissy had grinned and returned the next day with a pen wiper. Then a pair of magnifying glasses for reading.

"I don't need them," Sarah had said.

"Well, maybe Alex'll need them," Cissy said. "It's so far away, Sary—the railway doesn't even go all the way to Dillman. Getting supplies'll be hard."

"I know. So will friends." She had hugged Cissy, suddenly afraid. What if there were no women her age? Or no women at all? From her readings about the West, she knew it was filled with cowpokes and Indians and bull-whackers, people who drove the ox teams that carried supplies. There could be miles between ranches, the mountain lions were hungry, and the Indians still fierce, even if they were on reservations. The new *Beadle's Pocket Library* had told her a

20

lot about the West. Carefully, she tucked the lurid magazine under a petticoat, hiding it from Cissy's sharp eyes. CALAMITY JANE, screamed the 1885 headline, HEROINE OF WHOOP-UP. Below was a picture of a woman with wild, blowing hair and a fierce expression. Like me. She's wild like me, thought Sarah. Maybe I'll meet her, and then there'll be two heroines of whoop-up.

Then Cissy had hugged her with tears in her eyes, promised to write, and hurried down the path. Everyone wanted her to take more time, have new dresses made. But she wanted to leave *now*, with what she had, for a new life.

Remembering the good-byes, Sarah bound the coarse twine firmly around the crate and looked up as her aunt came in. Goody stood there, tall and straight, her mare's face quiet for once.

"Oh, Sary, you can change your mind—you don't *have* to go." She touched Sarah's shoulder. "Why don't I write to Mr. Proud telling him . . ."

"I'm not changing my mind, Goody." Sarah pushed her small horsehide trunk with the brass clasps off to one side. It was packed to the full: two workday dresses, one Sunday silk, two twill skirts, two white waists, two petticoats, one red flannel, two nightgowns, two sets of stays, a sweater, and a spring jacket. Her winter cloak hung on the wall peg, ready for the trip. It would be cold in Montana in mid-April. Mr. Proud had said so.

"I don't know what your ma'd say, you going off like this." Goody sighed and wrung her hands. "I don't think I can bear to come to the station."

Sarah looked at her with interest. She'd never seen anyone actually wring her hands, though she'd read of it. Goody's rough, big-knuckled hands twisted over and under each other.

"I could come visit you later," her aunt offered, "when the littles ones come. Though I don't know as I could stand the trip."

Sarah ran over and squeezed her tight. "Oh, Goody, don't work too hard and make sure you use the warming pan for your bed in the winter and don't let Pa make you do too much and if you need a hired girl, talk to Mrs. Black, she's got a niece who's looking for work." If she talked fast enough, then she wouldn't feel guilty.

"Is there anything else you haven't told me? Now you're going, makes me realize how much you did, Sary." Goody looked flustered, two gray curls springing from her cheeks. "The stove needs a new lid—that old rooster's ready for the cleaver—the peonies in front need manure—the roof has a small leak in front. . . ." She burst into tears and patted Sarah's hand, over and over.

The wagon rattled around to the side steps, and Pa jumped down. Together they loaded the trunk into the back.

"Write," Goody said, standing on the front step.

"I will." Sarah pulled on her cloak.

"Make sure you make a spring tonic from sassafras roots, *if* they have 'em out there, which I very much doubt."

"I will." Sarah felt ten years old.

"And don't let him boss you around too much; you're an American, Sary, not a cow. Here's something for your new home." Goody handed her a small cotton bag, filled with odd lumps and bulges. "Don't look till you get there—it's a surprise."

"Thank you." Sary tucked it into her satchel and kissed Goody. Pa handed her into the wagon and chirruped to the

22

horses. As the wagon rattled up the drive, her aunt called out something Sarah couldn't hear.

"What? Pa, stop the horses."

"Stop! I'm coming, too!" Goody shouted, waving frantically as she ran toward them. Pa held out a hand to her, Goody grabbed it, and pulled herself into the wagon. She breathed heavily and straightened her skirts. "Well? Get on, then, Frank, or you'll make Sary miss her train."

Sarah held her hand as they rode in silence up the road, up the rise to the main way. Sarah turned and looked back. Now the house didn't seem so small and tight; it seemed cozy, snugged in the shelter of a hill and protected by the two maples in front. The scilla Ma had planted so long ago would be out soon, blue against the winter brown grass. Would High Ridge have scilla?

Sarah felt small inside her cloak, younger than eighteen— too young to be married. Nonsense! she told herself. Martha Braman was married last year, and she was only seventeen. Grace Cooper got married at sixteen to that fat boy, Charlie Tower. Briefly, she wondered what happened on your wedding night. Goody's hints had not enlightened her on this matter. Just last night Goody had padded into her bedroom, candle in hand, gray braid hanging over her shoulder like a frayed rope.

"Sary?" Her aunt had sat on the bed and patted her knee. "There's things you should know, and with your ma being gone, no one's told you much."

Sarah sat up in bed. Five years ago Goody had told her about her monthlies and had mumbled that it had something to do with babies.

"You know when a man takes a wife they become—one

23

flesh." Goody fingered the quilt, and the candle threw wavering shadows on the wall. "One flesh," she repeated.

"I know, Goody," Sarah said gently. She had found out that somehow a man and woman put their bodies together, and from that babies came. Cissy said it was somewhat like horses, only different. Then she said it was like planting seeds—only different. All Sarah had seen once was Tillie Nelson—a no-account girl from Bickford—tussling with Jay Warner in the barn. There was a lot of fumbling with buttons, rustling, and heavy breathing, but that was all she was sure of. When she had told Cissy, her friend smiled uneasily and said it was important to marry a gentle man. But why?

"Oh, that's fine." Goody sighed. "To tell the truth, I don't know that much about it myself, 'cept for seeing animals breed. All I know is, the babies are worth it." She smiled and patted Sarah's cheek. And that was the extent of Goody's advice.

A cool wind whipped Sarah's hair into her eyes, and she tucked it under the special brown velvet hat made for the trip.

Goody glanced at her appraisingly. "Mr. Proud doesn't know how lucky he is. A fine young woman with all her teeth, plays the piano, sews, and does handiwork." She said the last uneasily. "And *certainly* has a way with animals." Of that there was no doubt; everyone knew Sarah could gentle a frightened horse or animal quicker than others.

"Almost there, Sary," Pa said, turning the horses toward the depot. The long, low building had a red roof, the pride of Dewborne. There was Mr. Black, the stationmaster, standing on the platform and holding up a large gold watch.

"On time?" Pa called out as he stopped the wagon.

24

"Six minutes late!" The walrus face shook sadly, betrayed by late trains and feckless conductors. Pa helped Sarah down and carried her trunk and crate to the platform. They looked pitifully small to Sarah—too tiny and insignificant to bear her so far away to a new life. Goody clambered down and stood guard over the luggage.

"Well, then, Sarah." Mr. Black smiled at her. "You're off to a new life, a husband, and a ranch."

"Yes, Mr. Black." Sarah adjusted her hat to a more rakish angle.

"I hope you'll be happy there, and so does Mrs. Black. She says she'll miss your talk at the ladies' sewing circle."

Missed, I'll be missed! Sarah thought. The whistle hooted in the distance and a black cloud chuffed along the horizon, closer and closer. Sound and light tumbling and grinding together—the hiss of steam, an acrid coal smell—and the sun glinting on impossibly bright wheels. The train screamed to a stop, and faces popped out the open windows.

"Maine's finest." Mr. Black beamed at them. "Horsehair and wool seats, brass fittings, polished walnut paneling." He extolled the train's many virtues as passengers stepped off and others boarded. A man with a wart on his nose took Sarah's trunk and boxes and put them in the baggage car.

Sarah, Pa, and Goody looked at each other, still stunned by the noise.

"All aboard . . . !"

"Write, Sary."

"I will, Pa."

"Come back if you don't like it!" he said. "We'll still be here." Goody was strangely silent, pursing and unpursing her lips.

Sarah began to cry and hugged her aunt, then Pa. She took in the smell of him for the last time—hay, chickens, and stale clothes. For that moment she loved him; he was home, all she knew.

He gripped her hands, forcing her away, and helped her up the steps.

"I'm not an old crone, Pa."

He responded by assisting her even more gravely, more slowly. "Watch that step—careful of that rail—"

Then she was through the door, the polished corridor stretching to one side. Pa stood below with a fixed smile on his face. An attendant closed the door and tipped his hat. The whistle hooted, the steam chuffed, and slowly, slowly the wheels began to grind, hauling the great black length down the tracks, protesting shrilly as they went. Still at the door, Sarah waved. Goody waved back and called out. Sarah cupped her ears and cried, "What?"

"*Be happy!*" shouted Goody.

"I'll try!"

Then, as the train gathered speed and the figures grew smaller on the platform, Pa lifted one black-clothed arm and moved it twice, back and forth.

CHAPTER FOUR

Sarah sat down on the seat and adjusted her velvet hat. It made her feel safe, contained, and she touched the brim again.

"Your first trip, is it?" asked a freckled young man opposite her with ginger hair.

"Well, not exactly my *first* trip." Sarah did not want to admit ignorance to a man whose pants didn't quite meet his socks.

"It's my first long trip." She squared her shoulders and leaned back against the seat. On either side were straight-backed seats covered with red wool. The windows gleamed in the sun, and clouds of black smoke rolled past. Red sparks coursed through the air, and the train swayed from side to side. Sarah put out a hand to steady herself, but her head seemed to rock inside. I am a mail-order bride. I am going West to be married. To someone I've never seen. What will I say to him? What will he say to *me?*

The ginger-haired man smiled at her. "I remember my first train ride when I was a boy—thought my nose'd bleed from the speed—thought the train'd fall apart. My aunt predicted certain ruin." He chuckled.

"And did it?" Sarah leaned forward.

"Did it fall apart? No. Did my nose bleed? No. But such details aren't meant for a young lady's ears."

The stout woman sitting beside the salesman—for Sarah

27

had seen the case, labeled TAYLOR'S BRUSHES, at his feet—sniffed with disapproval and pulled her young son closer.

Sarah smiled at him, and he grinned. "Where are you going?" he asked.

"Out West," Sarah answered. "Montana Territory. I'm to be married." The words dropped in her like stones down a well. They were so final.

The man leaned forward and balanced his elbows on his knees. "Montana Territory? That's out West, all right! Why, I had a cousin out there—worked at a stage depot—Charlie."

"Did he like it? Did he miss the East?"

"He liked it all right until he got himself killed." He rubbed his nose and coughed.

"How—killed?" All of Goody's worries rushed in. "Indians? The Sioux are on the reservation, but you never know—they're still wild. And there's mountain lions, of course, and grizzlies."

The stout woman nodded, and the cherries on her bonnet nodded with her. She hauled on her young son's sailor hat and said, "Yes, that's what I hear. Wild and ferocious. *Savages* still in spite of all our work to save 'em."

"Why, what have we done to save them?" Sarah asked, suddenly switching sides. Whatever that woman was for, she would be against.

"Sent out missionaries—opened up beautiful reservations—taught the savages to farm and keep animals—*civilization*, my dear child, Ca-*rist*-shun civilization!"

"Mmmph." Sarah rubbed a speck of dust off the lapel of her green jacket. "I'm not sure that'll save anyone, ma'am. I mean, *we* like farms and cows, but not everyone does, do they?"

"That's right," the young man agreed. "But I'd like to give farms and cows a chance. They say that the soil is nine feet deep out there and you can grow strawberries big as your fist. Peaches the size of a baby's head."

Sarah tapped her chin. "You never told us how your cousin was killed."

"Savages!" the woman said loudly. "Scalped, most likely."

"No, to tell the truth, Charlie died in a barroom brawl. Someone got mad, took out his pistol, and just started shooting. Poor Charlie was in the way."

"Drink!" The stout woman sniffed. "As bad as Indian savages. You hear that, Tommy?" She shook her son's arm. "That's the evils of drink for you."

"Yes'm," he said in a squashed voice.

"And you're to be married, then?" the woman asked. "I'm Mrs. Owens, by the way, and I do hope you're not marrying a railway man. They drink and gamble so."

"Oh, he's not a railway man." Sarah patted the letter in her bag. "He's a rancher."

With a quick glance at Sarah—taking in her youth, her new green jacket and soft hat—the woman guessed, "You one of those *mail-order* brides?"

Sarah nodded. The woman seemed to pull herself and her son farther away.

The man spoke up. "What's wrong with mail-order brides? It's a fine way for a man to get a wife. Works out as well as many a so-called love marriage."

Sarah smiled at him and sighed. Surely there must be other girls doing the same thing?

Then she noticed a young woman across the aisle who

winked at her. Sarah jerked her head up. She must have been mistaken. . . . *Women* didn't wink. But there it was again: a woman in a blue serge jacket and skirt, wearing a blue-trimmed hat. She winked again and leaned forward.

"I have a dear friend who went out as a mail-order bride last year—all the way to Kentucky."

"Oh?" Sarah turned toward her.

"Everything's just fine. Married a farmer and took on his two children. I think it's a fine thing you're doing."

Sarah sighed. "I'm glad you think so. Sometimes it seems awfully far away." The words seemed pale and weak compared to how she felt.

"The West always does, the first time." The woman smiled. "My name is Mary Burkett, and I'm going out to join my husband's family in northern Utah for a reunion. Most of the time, we're stationed at Fort Custer."

"Why, that's in Montana! What is it like? Is it awfully cold there in the winter? Does it get lonely? Do you like it there?" Sarah had to clamp her mouth shut, there was so much she wanted to ask.

A curious mix of pleasure and discontent passed over the woman's face. "Well, it's been cold *this* winter. Sometimes being an army wife is the finest thing in the world—new places, new people, new tales—and then there's the other times they don't tell you about. I lived in a tent for half a year with no window, and almost froze to death. We had one chair we used to toss a coin for." She laughed. "The big thing is not to lose your sense of fun. The ones that complain never last out West." She looked shrewdly at Sarah. "Somehow I don't think you'll be a complainer."

Sarah sat higher in her seat. Surely her face didn't show

what she was feeling—that she'd stepped off the edge of a ravine and was about to fall a thousand feet. Her stomach clutched in.

"Was it hard getting used to the West, Mrs. Burkett?"

"Please, call me Mary. Yes, it can be hard. The sky is different—big and empty. And the wind blows *all* the time. In summer the sun is so strong, it burns your skin up. And the winters!" Mary threw up her hands.

"Worse than Maine?"

"Blizzards that howl around your house. Freeze your skin, if you aren't careful. A girl can lose her looks awful fast out West." Mary patted her soft, white skin.

Sarah sat back in her seat. I don't have any looks to ruin, she thought. I'm not worried about that. Her stomach felt empty, almost queasy. What if he doesn't like me? What if I don't like *him?* With a mouth that felt dusty and dry, Sarah made a list in her mind. It wasn't completely unknown, what lay ahead. Number One: She would be in charge of all the food. Alex had said so. Number Two: In charge of all the cooking. I'll make my light buttermilk biscuits—my roast chicken—turkey with sage and onion stuffing, Goody's rec-ipe—that is, if I can *get* onions in Montana. I'll make flapjacks, eggs, sausage.

Sarah smoothed down the front of her jacket. Number Three: If there's a dairy, that will be my job, too. That's women's work. Number Four: Clothes. Ordering material, sewing up shirts and pants. Sarah's mouth felt like a desert. What if it's no better than Dewborne? What if all I do is chores from sunrise to sunset?

No. She shook her head. Alex had said he wanted some-one who could talk—and read. Said he had a library out there.

31

And I'll have a horse of my own—he said so. Maybe I can go look for Calamity Jane.

Sweating, Sarah took the worn, often-folded letter out of her bag. It was the second letter from Alex, sent before she'd written saying when she'd arrive. It struck her now that Alex had always assumed she'd come. Somehow, he didn't seem so far away, so unknown, if she called him Alex in her mind. She scanned the middle—the reassuring part.

"You can have your own horse, Miss Goodhue. The Western ones are tough and spirited."

She rustled the paper and read further down. "On Sundays we can take picnics down by the river and watch the sunset. My first wife, Ada, used to like that. Said it made her feel calm and rested."

Why did she need to feel calm?

"Or we can saddle up the horses and ride out to the pasture with the wild bluebells. Ada started a collection of pressed flowers, and I've gone on with it. Some think it not a man's work, but a man's got to have something to do out here besides stare at cows all day."

Sarah folded the letter up, trying to fold her worries inside the paper. What if she didn't measure up to this Ada? Sarah imagined a pale, willowy woman with smooth blond hair and a soft voice.

Well. She patted her hat. He'll just have to take me as I am. Sturdy—brown-haired—with a firm voice. And if he doesn't like me, I'll just . . . Sarah swallowed. I'll think of something else to do. There must be jobs out West for able-bodied young women. Because she couldn't go home again—not in defeat, not rejected.

"You're awfully quiet for a young woman making her

32

first trip West." Mary Burkett smiled gently.

"I'm sorry—I didn't mean to be rude. It's just that everything's so new, and I'm not sure what to expect. . . ." Her voice trailed off.

"Would you like to show me his picture?"

"Yes." Sarah handed her the daguerreotype, and Mary held it up to the light.

"Handsome, isn't he? Tall, well-built, looks like he has all his teeth."

"You sound just like my aunt."

"It's very important to have all your teeth. You'll like him, Sarah, I can tell. You wait—ranchers are the friendliest people in the world. It will be hard work out there, you know that, but you'll have fun. You wait."

Late in the afternoon, they arrived in Boston, clattering past red brick houses and tree-lined streets.

"Look, Mary—everything looks so *rich!*" There were gleaming horses and children in fur hoods led by governesses.

At the station, Mary took her arm and led her down the steps. "Across this platform—we change here for Chicago." She shouted to a porter, "Make sure Miss Goodhue's luggage is transferred to the Chicago train."

"What about yours?"

"I've only got this." Mary grinned and held up her satchel.

They washed their faces quickly in the station bathroom and dusted off their clothes. Then, up the steps of another black, shining train. Sarah felt blurred—like a picture whose edges had run—and was glad of Mary's arm.

33

"There." She piloted Sarah to a window seat and they sat down.

"Look." Sarah nudged Mary's arm. "There's old fire-and-brimstone."

Across the aisle, Mrs. Owens dragged her son into a seat and planted herself firmly on the aisle. The train started, and in the fading light, Sarah watched people take out box suppers and start to eat. She unpacked the cold chicken from home and shared it with Mary.

She watched the light fade into pink and green streaks, and saw lanterns lit in houses. Like tiny moons to light her way West. They comforted her. Later, an attendant came by and told them to follow him to the Pullman car. He led them through the rickety-clacking car, across a small swaying platform, into another car. Dark green curtains shielded the sleeping berths inside.

"Here you go, miss." The attendant grinned and swung her bag up into the netting strung over her bed.

"There's water at the end of the car—for rinsing your mouth and washing your face. And here's the ladder to your bed." He thwacked a rung on a small ladder built between the sleeping compartments.

"Well!" Mrs. Owens sniffed and thrust a broad shoulder between the green curtains of the berth below. "This is a nice howdy-do. Sleeping all jammed up like this. Won't do my lumbago any good, I can tell you."

Sarah looked at the shoe-button eyes and red face and considered slipping off the ladder and causing an unfortunate accident. Doom rolled out of that woman's mouth like the black clouds from the engine stack.

"I'm sure it's not as bad as it looks, Mrs. Owens. You're a woman of resource—I can see that—and you'll make do." She winked at the little boy peering out from behind his mother and climbed into bed.

Pulling the curtains tight, Sarah scrunched up on the flat hard bed and began to undress. Fourteen buttons for the green jacket. That took at least five minutes by her reckoning. Then, scrinching her arm around, she popped the buttons marching up her back—one-two-three, she breathed, and finally, fifteen! Sarah flung the white embroidered blouse into the net hammock.

"Darn clothes," she muttered. Why can't we dress like men? It wasn't that she wanted to *be* a man. She didn't. Or wear pants and loose jackets. She just wanted dresses that were easy to get in and out of, and cool—not all fitted with ruching, yards of grosgrain ribbon, multitudes of buttons—smaller than a baby's milk teeth—boots that took hours to hook up, pantalets, waists—

Sarah frizzed her side curls and bared her teeth. Now she was down to her white cotton vest and pantalets, her clothes heaped on one side.

There was a soft knock on the ladder outside. "Sarah? It's Mary. I wondered if you needed some help settling into your berth. I've done this so many times."

Sarah pulled the blanket around her and opened the curtain. "I can't seem to figure out where to put all my things!"

Mary reached in and began to arrange Sarah's clothes. "Skirt goes on the bottom, petticoats on top, *then* the jacket and the waist—then the hat. There." She smiled. "That's one thing you learn as an army wife—how to pack. Sleep well,

35

Sarah, and"—she patted her hand—"don't worry too much about the man you're to marry. I know many a rancher, and they're all fine fellows."

Was a fine fellow as good as a gentle man? What Cissy said she should marry? How could she ask a stranger all the things she wanted to know, all the things Goody had hinted at but been helpless to answer?

"But I *do* worry. What if he doesn't like me? What if I don't like him?"

"Well, there's many a marriage based on love that's gone wrong, Sarah. I've seen it happen. Sometimes the best marriages are between friends. You can *learn* to like almost anybody."

Sarah rubbed her nose with the blanket. "I hope you're right."

Mary smiled and said, "I know I'm right. Now, sleep well and sweet dreams." She withdrew her head, and Sarah heard her heels clicking down the corridor. From below, she could hear Tommy complaining.

"But Ma, why do I haf'ta wear a nightshirt? There's no sense in it. I'll just wear my pants. . . ."

"Oh, no you don't, young man. We're keeping to *civilized* ways here."

Sarah chuckled and pulled on her nightdress. Outside the window, a golden moon rose over dark trees. A river gleamed silver as they rattled beside it. Someone started to snore, started-stopped, started-stopped. Then it was quiet. Sarah got under the covers—clean sheets that smelled of bleach and one harsh gray blanket—and pulled them up to her chin. Somewhere someone sang softly. "Goin' on the *night* train/Back *home* again . . ."

The wheels clickety-clacked, clickety-clacked—the dark rustled with all the sleepers behind their green curtains—and Sarah fell asleep, dreaming of a vast ranch covered with grazing cattle with Alex and her in the middle, astride their horses. And somewhere out of sight, Calamity Jane slept under the stars, wild and free.

CHAPTER FIVE

The towns blurred together. Little towns with houses clustered along black rivers. Bigger towns with brash red mills and ringing bells. Lonely farms plunked in the middle of gray-white fields. Children in mufflers who waved as the train hooted by. Stained depots like false teeth forgotten on a night table. Sarah and Mary rode and slept, ate and slept, and tried to keep their clothes clean from the ever-present cinders and ash. Sarah reread the letters from Alex another ten times and tried not to worry.

In Chicago, the salesman left and waved good-bye, wishing Sarah good luck, and Mrs. Owens and her son departed in a cloud of complaints. Then on for another long day and night, the train puffing and straining as they reached the mountains of Wyoming the following day. The train stopped at the top of one peak, where she and Mary poked their heads out a window and breathed the frigid, thin air. The mountains fell away, sharp and blue.

This is what Montana will be like, Sarah promised herself. New, clean, and full of promise.

The train clanked down to the plains, brakes screeching, and they chuffed over miles of snowy, desolate grasslands with only the telegraph poles against a bleak sky for company.

At the end of the fifth day, they stopped in a small town in northern Utah to change trains.

"What a godforsaken place," Mary Burkett whispered to

Sarah at the top of the train's steps. Below was a platform and a depot that seemed built by a demented child. Strange protuberances bulged over the windows, gable ends popped out of nowhere, and gingerbread fringe galloped around the roof edges.

Sarah giggled. "Must 'of been drunk when they built it," she whispered back.

"Drunk or crazy," Mary said, and hopped off the train.

The rest of the passengers straggled off and stood wanly on the platform. Sarah knew how they felt.

"I'm not sure my legs still work." She tried a quick two-step and sniffed the air. Cold and dry with a bite to it. Dusty enough to taste on the tongue, like licking wool. She coughed. "What do we do now?"

Mary smiled thinly. "I know what to do—I've made this trip twice before. We go to Mrs. Laynor's Lodgings for tonight and leave at dawn tomorrow. We'll leave our trunks and crates here in the depot."

Sarah gripped her satchel and followed Mary down a wide, dusty street. There was a greengrocer's called Harold's, a dry-goods store featuring bits of rope, one saloon with a broken window, and a few houses of a gray and discouraged character.

Mary led the way down the street. Sarah thought sadly of her snug farm in Dewborne, and the settled look of houses that have grown into the land and hills. The freezing wind whipped their skirts around their ankles and blew stinging dust into their eyes. Sarah heard a cow moo and saw a girl in a frayed shawl carrying a pail to a gray house. The girl sang in a piping voice, "Mary had a lit-tle lamb, lit-tle lamb, lit-tle lamb. . . ."

Sarah shivered and pulled her cloak closer. The sound made the sky seem even wider and emptier and the wind colder. Suddenly, she wished Goody were here with her sense and her calm size; *she'd* fill up that empty sky. Sarah felt teary and pulled her hat brim lower as Mary hurried up the steps under the sign MRS. LAYNOR'S LODGINGS and knocked on the door. It opened swiftly, and a buxom woman with two teeth held out her arms.

"Come in, come in, you poor souls. Famished, no doubt! Tired, it goes without saying. Grimy and gritty from that dreadful train ride."

And leading them up narrow, cold stairs, she continued to describe their journey for them. "Untold stops. Long waits. Crying babies in corridors. Women with the vapors. Men with hip flasks, *which*"—she turned and frowned—"we don't like to mention, but it's a fact of life out here—a fact of life. We try to get them to take the pledge, but it's uphill work, girls."

She opened the door to a small bedroom and showed them in. "You'll have to share a room, as I'm full up with men going out to Oregon and California." Mary thanked her as she left.

Sarah surveyed the room: two rickety bedsteads, faded blue coverlets, and pictures from *Godey's Lady's Book* of majestic women in feathered hats. She went to the window and looked out at a brown and white land that stretched away to the horizon. It rippled in waves like the sea, and she could see nothing on it—not a bird or animal or a human being.

"Nothing!" Sarah said.

"What did you say?" Mary splashed water in the china basin and washed her face vigorously.

40

"Nothing." Sarah turned and saw that the water in the basin was gray.

Mary threw it out the window and poured fresh for Sarah. "It gets in your skin, this dust." Mary scrubbed her face with the towel, unpinned her hair, and brushed it. "I wonder if it's dusty in High Ridge?"

Sarah washed, combed her bangs, and tried not to think of Montana Territory. It couldn't be so thin and gray and empty. Sour with unfinished houses and streets with nowhere to go. *Worse than Dewborne*, a voice said inside.

"Come on." Mary touched her arm. "I know what you're thinking. You've got greenhorn sadness all over your face. It will get better. It looks empty, I'll grant you. But the friends you make out here are the best you'll ever find. And the land?"

Mary smiled and pinned her hair into a coil on her neck. "Well, the land makes its own friends, you'll see."

A bell rang, and Sarah followed Mary downstairs to the main room. There were two trestle tables set up and people already crowded around them. The cookstove was in a pantry next to the dining room, and Sarah could see two young girls hustling back and forth with plates and saucers and bowls of steaming mashed potatoes.

"Chicken," Mrs. Laynor announced, plunking a roasted bird on each table. "Bread and beans. Come on, girls, don't be shy." She waved them to a seat. "Dig in."

Sarah winced. Would she end up talking like that after a year out West, like some—some army sergeant?

Mary nudged her and nodded at the pantry. Sarah saw a big kettle with steam puffing out of it. One of the young girls held a fistful of dirty knives and forks in the steam, then wiped them hastily on her grimy apron.

41

Sarah choked and looked at her fork. Quickly, she scrubbed it on the inside of her jacket edge while Mary chuckled. Then she ate. Stringy chicken and thin gravy with stale bread and ancient butter. She ate quickly, so as not to taste, and thought longingly of Goody and Pa at home eating supper without her. Maybe they were missing her, finding it hard to run the farm without her. What kind of person would go off and leave an aging aunt and father to fend for themselves? Selfish, that's what she was, selfish.

Talk clattered around her. "A man can get rich out there—just toss the seeds in the air—climate's good for the lungs, too—"

Another man said, "Oregon's the place to go, boys, I'm going out there, staking my claim. Soon's you know, we'll be riding in buggies and buying silk."

The men talked and talked, beards bunching under the words, eyes eager.

"Reminds me of the cows coming home," Sarah whispered to Mary.

"What does?" Mary stopped midbite.

"The men, rushing into something, looking for the best hay, the best stall . . ."

Mary grinned. "I know, they're just full of themselves, but *someone's* got to settle the West. They're the best we've got."

Sarah watched gravy dribble down a blond man's chin and wondered, Was he the best they had? And why did the West need people like him?

At the end of dinner, Mrs. Laynor bid them rise and sing a temperance hymn. They all said their good-nights and filed upstairs to their bedrooms. Sarah imagined the men lying side

42

by side like sardines on the floor, as she saw ten go through one door. Their own room was icy, and little drafts blew the curtains out from the windows. Teeth chattering, Sarah pulled her winter nightgown over her head and began to undress beneath it. Across the room, Mary did the same. What would happen if they actually *saw* each other's bare arms and legs? She giggled, her mouth covered by flannel.

"What's the matter?" Mary struggled under her nightgown, making odd bulges and corners.

"It's just so silly. Here we are—tired beyond belief—undressing in a tent!" She stuck her head through the yoke. "Mary?" Her voice wavered.

"Mmm?"

"Mary, if *we* are too shy to undress in the light, what will happen when I marry?"

Mary sat on the bed, frowning as she unbuttoned her dusty boots. "Well, Sarah, I can't really tell you what it is like. No one can. You'll just have to find out for yourself." Briskly, she unpinned her hair, brushed and plaited it for the night.

"And your Mr. Proud is probably a bit older than you, been married before. That should help."

Help what? Sarah wanted to shout. Help me or him? And why do we *need* help? She got into bed and turned down the lamp, until the flame died. It seemed there was a vast conspiracy around marriage—not to tell you what it was like or what to expect. She wriggled angrily inside the bed, and her toes bumped a warm brick wrapped in flannel. Mrs. Laynor's kindness. And she remembered something Goody had said just before she left.

"Try to keep that tongue of yours gentled, Sarah. Don't

be so quick to judge out West. Wait until you *know* them before you declare them fools."

" 'Night, Sarah." Mary rustled in her bed.

" 'Night, Mary." She tucked her nose under the covers and wondered what Alex was thinking that very moment. Was he nervous—as she was? Or was he reading books and looking after his cattle and being calm as the day is long?

CHAPTER SIX

The next morning the train left in a whirl of gritty snow, and all Sarah could see of the town were the gray tips of houses poking up. She felt depressed and raw, as if the snow were an ill omen for her journey. And it did not help that Mary was preparing to leave at the next stop—smoothing down her coat front, moistening her curls and patting them into place, gripping the handle of her bag.

The train began to slow in small jerks and rattles. Mary rose and cleared her throat.

"Well, Sarah?"

"Well, Mary?"

"Everything'll be all right. Don't worry—it ruins the complexion. Don't stay out in the summer sun, and watch out for that dratted *wind*—it rips your washing to shreds." The buildings of a small depot slowed to a stop outside the windows. Mary lifted her satchel. "Don't be afraid. There's nothing to be afraid *of*." She hugged Sarah tightly and then shrieked.

"Will! There he is, look!" She pointed to a tall, blond man standing on the platform. He tipped his hat to them and held out his arms.

"Hush, now, hush." Mary dabbed her eyes. "I'll write—promise to write, Sarah, whenever you feel lonely and even if you aren't. Maybe we can visit." She hugged her again and ran down the steps into the arms of her husband.

He rubbed his beard against Mary's cheek, making her shriek again, picked her up and carried her to their sleigh, and dumped her in the seat. He jumped in, flicked the reins, and the runners slid over the packed snow. Sarah's last glimpse of Mary was of her heels in the air, hat skewered sideways, laughing and waving blindly at the train.

Sarah was glad her green jacket was unbuttoned. She felt so sad, she thought her buttons'd pop off if the jacket was done up. She had had enough of waving good-bye and enough of people giving her advice.

Sarah adjusted her hat, pinned it firmly to her hair, and stared out the window. The train started up again, *chuff-chuff*, *chuff-chuff*, and clattered over the tracks. Far away the tracks seemed to meet in a point and then were erased by the sky.

Sarah remembered a teacher telling them one day, "Columbus's men almost mutinied because they believed they would sail over the edge of the world and fall into dragons' mouths." She'd laughed then, but now it seemed the train would steam over the edge of the horizon and fall into space. She felt a little dizzy. Goody and Pa seemed farther and farther away—unreachable with all that sky and prairie and long track between her and them.

I-am-a-mail-order-bride. She attached each word to a telegraph pole going by. I-am-a-parcel-being-sent-to-an-un-known-person. I-shall-be-unwrapped. She shifted in her seat and chewed on a thumb. Unwrapped—and then what? Don't-think-about-it. Don't-think.

For the rest of the day, she stared at the white grasslands and watched the light fade. From time to time, she took out Alex's picture and peered at it, but each time it reassured her less. He seemed remote and tall. She would be dwarfed by him. He'd think she was too young—or too plain. And again and again, she came back to the image of a parcel being unwrapped, and then what?

When the light was gone, the train slowed and clanked to a stop in Red Rock, Montana Territory. "All out," the conductor called. "End of the line, ladies and gents. The railroad don't go no further."

"Doesn't," Sarah muttered, "doesn't go *any farther.*"

"Let me help you with that, miss." A young man took her satchel and helped her down the steps. "Well, here we are in Montana Territory and it's hooves or feet from now on." He spread his arms wide and breathed in. "That air just makes a man want to stand up straighter."

Sarah took a deep breath. No dust this time. Cool, thin air, with a hint of woodsmoke, and a dark sky sprinkled with stars.

"Now," the man shepherded her into the tiny depot. "Are you being met?"

Sarah shook her head.

"Taking the stagecoach?"

"Yes."

"This way then, out this door." He strode through to the other side of the platform, where a battered coach waited. It had been fitted with runners for the snowy roads. Passengers were already inside and seated on top.

He made sure her trunk was tightly roped on top, handed her in, and said to the driver, "Careful, Charlie, you've got ladies this time out." He tipped his hat.

Sarah smiled through the window. In the lantern's light she saw his eyes. Nice. And a firm mouth and ears a mother'd be proud of. But not as nice as Alex's. She touched the pho-

47

tograph again and waved as the stagecoach lurched over the trail.

"It couldn't be called a road," complained an older woman in a sagging yellow bonnet.

"Ma'am, none of the roads in Montana Territory can be called roads. You ain't back East, ma'am," said a man in an army uniform.

She complained again, a wordless mutter. The other two inside passengers, an older man and a fashionable young woman in a feathered hat, drew their coats about them and sighed. The yellow bonnet kept up a low-toned complaint. "Roads—my age—rheumatism in the joints—mmm, mmm."

"Oh, Lord." The army man reached inside his coat. "Here, you better have some of this—it's going to be a long trip." He offered a small bottle.

The woman held out a hand in mock protest, and then daintily took the flask and tipped it to her lips. Sarah watched her swallow, and swallow, and swallow.

"Here!" He made a grab for the bottle. "That's got to last the trip, lady. Go easy on it. You don't want any, miss, do you?" He peered at her in the faint light. "You seem too young for this."

Sarah shook her head and took a shawl out of her satchel. Folding it twice, she tucked it between her cheek and the stagecoach side. Maybe she could get some sleep. The driver had said they wouldn't reach Dillman until tomorrow night, and that was without any long stops. The cold gnawed at her shoulders, and she wrapped the cloak more tightly about her.

The coach jolted and creaked, and Sarah swayed from side to side. She dreamed that they all were in a vast, bumpy swing—people, luggage, and horses, swaying in a cold wind.

48

And Calamity Jane was pushing the swing, pushing and laughing. She woke, and slept, and woke again.

At dawn, they stopped for food and a change of horses at a tiny log cabin. Sarah stepped out and stretched her aching legs. The sky was red and clear. Somewhere a coyote howled, "*Yip-yip-yip-yowww!*" A small child with a smudged face and tattered dress peered out of the cabin window. At a rough plank table, they had tough beef and "double-folded bread." Mary had warned her about it. "Have to fold it double, Sarah, to cover up the taste of the rancid butter." With tough beef and bitter coffee, that was breakfast. It did not warm Sarah, and the cold seemed to have settled into her back like a row of teeth.

Then on again. By now the woman in the yellow bonnet and the army man were sprawled across the coach, snoring. Sarah looked outside at a white-and-brown land with tall blue mountains in the distance. *Her* mountains?

Maybe she would see some Indians, black hair streaming in the wind, horses trotting swiftly. She had not seen one real Indian yet on the whole trip, except for that sorry bunch somewhere in Utah, huddled next to a hotel. They had looked smudged and tired, like coins used so often all the shine had worn off. Better yet, maybe she would see Calamity Jane, whooping it up, riding pell-mell across the land, waving her hat, and yelling just for the joy of it.

They lurched and swayed across the snowy prairie, through a shallow black river, past bent pines. As the light paled, Sarah shoved the window down and looked out. The cold air pushed at her, and yellow bonnet complained.

"Shut that window, do—want to give us nee-monia?"

There, not far away, rising up out of the horizon—Ma's

mountains. They were immense, almost frightening, and they made her feel small and even colder. She closed the window and waited. Soon she would be there. Soon she would be married—to a stranger. She pressed down on her thoughts, but they kept popping out. What if he's mean? What if he doesn't like me? What if he's changed his mind? She counted the money in her snap purse. Twenty dollars from Pa. That would pay for a hotel room for a bit, if Alex weren't there. She could always get a job cooking or working in the hotel— or maybe on a ranch. She snapped and unsnapped the purse until yellow bonnet complained, "My nerves! *If you don't mind.*"

One hour later, reckoned by the watch pinned to her lapel, the stagecoach stopped by a gray building. The driver opened the door and Sarah stepped down, every muscle aching in her backside. "Stand straight," she told herself. "You're to be a bride now—don't let him see you stooping. Where *is* he?" It was hard to see in the dark and the flickering light of the lanterns.

People spilled off the coach, talking and laughing, and were kissed and hugged by others. The passengers on top, in coats and blankets, could barely climb down and complained bitterly of the cold. Sarah searched the small group outside the hotel. Three homesteaders—it looked like—in denim overalls and poor cloth coats. None was Alex. A family welcomed the fashionable young woman, who kept patting her hair. A coughing man climbed down from the outside seat of the coach and kissed his wife and baby—probably had consumption and had come out for the prairie cure. A man in a heavy coat and hat with a dog at his knee waited off to the side. She took out the photo and looked at the man, who

50

came up and asked, "Miss Goodhue? I am Alex Proud."

Sarah nodded, unable to speak. He was huge. Enveloped in a bearskin coat. The hat hid his face. All she could see was a moustache and what might be a smile. She felt dizzy from the long, jolting trip and stumbled.

He took her arm and led her into the hotel, inquiring gently, "Are you tired? You must be hungry. Would you like to freshen up upstairs and then have some supper?" The dog followed at his heels.

"Yes, yes, I would like that." He asked how she felt! That was courteous, that showed a warm heart.

Inside the hotel, a potbellied stove warmed a bare room with four tables. "Upstairs, Miss Goodhue. I've reserved Room Number Five for the night."

Wearily, Sarah climbed the bare stairs to the room and opened the door. Her room or *their* room? How were these things done? Sarah's hands trembled as she combed her hair and washed her face. It was a pity she was so plain. She dabbed a little cornstarch on her nose, as Goody had told her to, and used the chamber pot. She covered it and tucked it under the bed, worrying. No one had told her what to do about these intimate details.

Downstairs, at the table, Alex had ordered her a pot of tea and some dinner. He helped her into a chair. She touched the flank of the dog with her shoe.

"Now. First, I thought we'd take some dinner. Then, if it suits you, we can be married right away. I've spoken to Reverend Brown and he's in the hotel. We can spend the night here and travel out to our ranch in the morning. How does that sound, Miss Goodhue?"

Sarah hesitated. She thought he smiled, but it was hard

to see under his hat. All she could see in the shadow was his salt-and-pepper moustache. How odd!

"That sounds just fine," she said finally, "and thank you for being so thoughtful." Not like Pa, who never once in all his life asked if she were cold or hot or hungry.

Did he find her unattractive? Sarah sipped mournfully at her tea. Was that why he kept his hat on? But he had said "our ranch," and that warmed her. She looked at his hands. They were brown and worn. Maybe he is in his late thirties, Sarah thought, or a bit more. Of course, hands do get rough from the sun and hard ranch work. Goody had said, "Expect a wrinkled man. That sun is harsh."

He chatted gently and easily throughout the meal—about "their" cattle, "their" ranch, and his plans for the summer. Sarah answered from time to time, trying to see his face under the hat, but shadows covered his features.

"Well, then, if you're through." He rose and Sarah rose quickly, tipping the chair over. It clattered to the floor and heads turned.

"Sorry," Sarah murmured, but Alex picked it up, patted her arm, and led her into an adjoining room. The dog clicked at their heels. The parlor was cold as a Maine wind and decorated with bilious green wallpaper. Pictures of shipwrecks hung on the walls. A man in a black coat stood and adjusted his spectacles.

"Ah, Mr. Proud, here you are with the young bride-to-be." He seemed to pull his smile out of his breast pocket and then return it quickly.

Sarah clasped her hands. I won't be nervous, I won't get sick to my stomach. Everything'll be fine. Mary said so.

"Now, please stand over here." Reverend Brown motioned them in front of a shiny black sofa. There was a large camera positioned opposite. "Take your places and repeat after me. Do you want that dog in here, Mr. Proud?"

"Of course. He's my best man." Alex chuckled, and Sarah thought about smiling but didn't.

"Alex, will you have this woman to be thy lawful wedded wife?" He nodded to Alex who said, "I do."

"Sarah, will you have this man to be thy lawful wedded husband?" He nodded at her.

Sarah hesitated. *Why* didn't Alex take his hat and coat off? Was he sick? Was she marrying an eccentric or someone with nee-monia? She began to smile and said, "I do," quickly, before the smile went.

At the end, Alex slipped a gold band on her finger and kissed her hand—not her cheek.

A photographer rushed in on them and took up his position behind the camera. He fussed, "Mr. Proud, please *take* that hat off just for the photograph. We know you ranchers don't like to be bareheaded, but just this once."

Sarah sighed. It was all right. It must be the custom out here. She almost giggled.

Alex took his hat off slowly, shyly, and did not look at her. Sarah felt her stomach clutch in. His hair was white, snow-white, and sparse on top. The man was old! Not edging-into-his-fifties old, or just merely worn-out-from-use-at-forty old—but white-bushy-eyebrows old, skin-like-a-brown-wrinkled-map old. That's why the hat, the greatcoat. A disguise.

"Smile!" said the photographer. "And don't move."

Sarah smiled at the black bump of the photographer, at the pictures of sinking ships, as the flash pan went off and blinded her and the dog howled.

CHAPTER SEVEN

Sarah still saw spots and stars from the flash. Alex led her up the stairs and halted by Room No. 5. He tipped his hat.

"Mrs. Proud? A good-night to you. I'll be down the hall—thought you'd like the rest this evening," he said hurriedly. "Sleep well, and sweet dreams."

He walked down the corridor, his dog beside him, and Sarah let herself into the room. She unpinned her hat and flung it on the bed. Didn't need to worry about being plain! She stamped around the room, tearing her clothes off.

"Good God Almighty, what have you gotten yourself into, Sarah Goodhue?" She sat on the bed, covered her face with her hands, and rocked back and forth. An old man. At the end of his life. Probably'll need nursing in a year or two. Sarah shuddered and got into bed. She rolled over, bunching the blankets. Could she get out of this? Back to Goody and Pa by the fire at home? It may have been dull, but at least no one had lied. And there was always the hope that something better was around the corner or down the road, out of sight.

Sarah rolled over again and poked her nose out of the covers. The air was raw and still. Outside, a sharp moon hung in the sky. She couldn't go back home—admit failure to the whole town—to Cissy, Dan Monroe, all the ladies of the sewing circle. Besides, she knew nothing about the law—how to get a divorce. Could you get a divorce on grounds of deception? What would Calamity Jane do? Shoot him? Or just leave?

The Hotel Comfort creaked in the wind. Sarah could hear bedsprings groaning as neighboring sleepers turned over. Someone talked about turnips. Sarah lay on her stomach and buried her face in the pillow. When she'd been sick at home, Goody always brought a cup of camomile tea to her bedside. She imagined Goody now, standing near in her long nightgown, gray braid over one shoulder. "Drink up!" she'd say. "You'll feel better in the morning."

At the thought of Goody, Sarah remembered the present stuck so hurriedly into her satchel at the start of the journey. She struck a match, lit the lamp, and opened the bag. Inside was the cotton sack. Sarah reached inside and pulled out something smooth and moist. Dirt clung to her fingers. She held a knobby circle in her hand, then pressed it to her cheek. Scilla! Goody had dug up Ma's bulbs for her new home. Packed in dirt, they had stayed damp, and some showed a few small green shoots and white roots.

Sarah remembered planting them long ago. She had been small, in a blue pinafore and black buttoned boots. Ma had knelt by the newly dug flower bed and let Sarah poke a hole with a stick for each bulb. Together, they tucked the scilla deep in the earth, and Ma told her how they lay sleeping through winter, waiting for spring.

Sarah began to cry, holding the sack to her chest. Sobbing, she got into bed and pressed her nose into the fabric. Goody had touched this. Earth from the farm was inside.

"Oh, Ma. What have I done? What am I going to *do*?"
She blew her nose, coughed, and stared into the dark.

Holding the bulbs tight, she finally slept and dreamed of mountains she trudged up without ever reaching the top.

The next morning she looked out at the whirling snow and pulled on knit stockings, two petticoats—one flannel— her heaviest skirt, and a warm jacket. She cracked the ice in the washbasin and splashed water on her face. Her hair was pinned up in seconds, and taking a deep breath, she marched downstairs.

Alex was already sitting at the table beside the stove. He rose and held out a chair for her.

"Well, Mrs. Proud, and how did you sleep?"

"A bit restless, Mr. Proud, a bit restless." If I repeat everything twice, Sarah thought, I can fill up the spaces.

He pushed her chair in gently and sat down. "It's angry weather out there." He gestured to the hotel windows.

Angry weather? What about the angry weather *inside?* How could she live with a person who had so cheated and deceived her? Her foot nudged the dog, who was already curled under the table. She felt its warm face against her stocking.

"Do you always travel with your dog?" she asked.

"*Always.* Blitzen always comes with me."

She peered underneath the table and saw the solid, yellow head of the dog resting on two large paws.

"Big dog, isn't he?" she said.

"Mmm, yes, you need a large dog out West."

And, God willing, talk. What kind of conversation was this, about dogs and weather?

Outside, a stiff wind blew two men across the street and made a horse skitter sideways at a hitching post. Gray, hard-looking flakes spun down.

They sat awhile in silence, a scratchy silence as uncomfortable as new woolens. Sarah watched the other guests—a stout man in a green coat with a shiny watch chain and two pasty-faced daughters. A woman with tired hair set down a pot of tea and a plate of flat eggs before Sarah.

"Will we be able to travel today?" Sarah asked.

"Don't see why not." Alex sipped his coffee. "It'll be cold in the sleigh, but I've got to get back to my beeves."

Sarah smiled in spite of herself. She imagined a corral of hefty steers waving their hooves as Alex came home, mooing a welcome.

"Do they always miss you when you're away?" she asked. "Do they pine and write sentimental couplets?" She had determined at least to try and be polite.

Alex pushed back his chair. "Why, Mrs. Proud, you didn't tell me you had a sense of humor." He smiled. "They write songs for me when I'm away, the beeves do. Plan on publishing them one day."

He pulled out a small leather pouch, took two quarters from it, and left them on the table. "Dress warmly, Mrs. Proud. It's a day's drive to the ranch, and that wind is sharp."

Keep your mind on that—the ranch, the cattle. Don't think about that white hair shining in the lamplight when the hat was swept off. Don't think about how he didn't look at you when the preacher pronounced you man and wife. Sarah ran upstairs, glad they were going. She didn't know if she could bear another day at the Hotel Comfort. She'd left nothing in the room—"my wedding room," she said aloud. The words sounded dry and hard. Quickly, Sarah peered in the mirror. Plain—plain as the day is long. It's no wonder I wound up married to an old man. At least he didn't share my room last night; that showed some kindness, she guessed. She pinched her cheeks to make them red, put on another jacket, her winter cape and hat, and tied it down with a thick scarf.

Alex was waiting by the door. "There you are, and warmly dressed. Good." He took her satchel and directed one of the hotel boys to put her trunk and crate in the sleigh outside. The dog stood patiently to one side.

"Up you go." He helped her into one side of the sleigh and swung up on the other. Bundled up though he was, Sarah saw that he moved easily and not stiffly like an old man. The woman from the hotel bustled out and handed her a warm brick wrapped in cloth. "For your feet, Mrs. Proud." Alex tucked a bearskin robe around their legs and middles. "Now, you come back and see us soon," the woman said. "It can get pretty lonely out there on those ranches. Mr. Proud, you bring your wife in here for a nice chat one of these days."

He nodded and said, "Get up." The two sturdy bays trotted down Main Street, and Blitzen followed, head low. The wind blew in their faces and the snow stung Sarah's eyes.

"Is it safe?" she asked through her muffler.

"What?"

"Is it *safe*?"

"Oh, yes," he shouted back. "The snow's not bad—it won't amount to much. It's the wind that hurts."

Sarah nodded and peered ahead. A gray-brown prairie unrolled like a rumpled blanket. No houses. A bumpy line of barbed wire. And in the distance was something large and dark, hidden by the snow. It must be the mountains. Could mountains make up for what had happened?

They trotted and walked, trotted and walked, and when they were cold, they got off and ran beside the horses. Sarah's

58

feet were numb when she sat, and when she ran they felt as if live coals were in her shoes.

The falling snow didn't seem to bother the horses. They plodded on, as if on a main road in sunny June, drawn by their barn and hay. Sarah lost track of time. Although Alex had tucked the bearskin robe tightly about her, she felt like a piece of luggage—hard, lumpy, and stiff.

"Are you all right, Mrs. Proud?" he asked frequently. "Keeping warm?" And Sarah would bare her teeth, imitating a smile, and then realize he could not see through her muffler. "Yes," she shouted each time. "All right."

Later, the snow changed from a gray-white to something invisible in a charcoal sky. It fell harder, and the wind swirled around them. It was like a wolf prowling beside, tearing at her muffler and snapping at her eyes. Her eyes teared up and then froze shut. When she tried to open them, they would not. "Alex!" she shouted. But he did not hear. Carefully, she held her muffler over her eyes and picked the lashes open. Her stomach squeezed in. The sleigh began to lurch from side to side, and Alex got down again to walk beside the horses. The dog still trotted patiently behind them. Sarah clutched the seat with numb fingers; how much longer? Did this man even know where they were? If he'd lied about his age, why not lie about being a rancher, too?

She imagined the letter to Pa:

Dear Mr. Goodhue,

We are sad to report the death of your daughter, Sarah Goodhue, recently Mrs. Proud. Due to a late spring blizzard, she and her husband never arrived at the ranch, but were found frozen stiff, still sitting, in the sleigh.

Yours in sorrow,
The Hotel Comfort

Sarah pushed herself off the sleigh and stomped on her feet. She trotted up beside Alex and shouted, "Are we lost?" The wind burned her cheeks and mouth, and Sarah hastily pulled her scarf up.

"Don't worry," came through Alex's muffler. "Soon there."

They trotted stiffly beside the horses as darkness and snow closed around them. She felt groggy and drugged from the cold. Uphill—Sarah could feel the ground sloping under her feet—and then, dark lines crossed ahead, and there was a smudge of yellow.

Alex turned the horses' heads and brought them to a stop. "Inside," he shouted. "Get inside." He took the horses and sleigh off into the darkness.

Sarah stumbled up to the yellow light and a door opened. She fell inside. Something small and warm held her up.

"Poor thing," it murmured. Maybe it was a lamp, Sarah thought groggily, a talking lamp. It unwrapped her scarf, pulled off her hat and cape, and led her to a roaring fire. The heat hurt her eyes. She felt the dog go past her to the fire.

"Here, sit." She was pushed into a chair and a basin of steaming water appeared at her feet. The small person stripped off her snowy boots and stockings and put her feet in the basin. Sarah cried out, but two hands held her feet under the water until they stopped hurting and warmth seeped into her icy toes. The dog leaned against her leg and whined.

The door banged and Alex came in and shed his coat on the floor. He came over to the fireplace and knelt down. "How is she?" he said to the person.

"Tired and cold, but she be all right. Not delicate flower like other one." The small being handed a cup of hot tea to

Alex and one to Sarah. She could smell the whiskey in it.

"Drink up!" he said. "Drink." And she did, the heat flowing down and chasing out the dull, gray cold.

"It was . . . the sky," she said.

"Hmm?" Alex patted her knee.

"The sky . . ." She couldn't say that the sky had invaded and chilled her even more than the wind and snow. And only the whiskey-laced tea could chase it away.

Then, hardly aware of the room or the people, Sarah was carried off to bed and tucked under a mountain of blankets to dream of wagons and horses and photographers in black suits who popped out, commanding her to smile!

CHAPTER EIGHT

Something scraped the wall behind her ear. Sarah turned over and buried her face in the pillow. Wolves—coyotes? *Swish—swish—swish*, the sound went on. Her toes were cold and her shoulder blades ached where the top blanket had fallen back.

She didn't want to open her eyes, to see what she had married. It could be a bare log cabin with snow on the floor. She could be all alone with a man who called her Mrs. Proud and always wore a hat. How would she get through this day? When she thought of the wedding, her teeth grated together. Then she thought of the frozen, bleak ride across the prairie. This wasn't Maine—this was freeze-your-eyelids-together country. This was wind-like-a-wolf country.

Once, she'd watched Pa butcher a pig back home. Pa had struck the pig first on the head before he'd shot it. She remembered the stunned look on the pig's face. I feel the same, she thought.

Sarah rose on one elbow, eyes sore and tender. She was alone in a small bedroom with log walls. Her clothes hung on a nearby hook, and her boots were placed neatly underneath. Someone had undressed and put her in a white flannel nightgown. Alex? The other person? On a stand by the bed was a china pitcher with a cloth laid over it. Sarah lifted it and looked inside. Frozen.

There was one window, and it was blizzard-white. Gritting her teeth, Sarah swung her legs out of bed, howled, grabbed her clothes, and pulled them under the covers. "Cold! Mary—you didn't tell me it could be s-so c-c-cold!" First the gray stockings, then the flannel petticoat, the wool skirt, the woolen vest, the waist, then the jacket. All that weaseling around in the train berth had done some good, she thought. Taught me to get dressed inside a peapod.

She got out of bed and pulled on her boots. "Ooh!" Little pockets of frozen air settled on her toes. Where *was* everybody? She pushed open the door and went into a main room. It was filled with a cold, gray light. Quickly, she noted the shelves on the wall filled with volumes—Alex's library; a Winchester rifle over the door; two blank white windows; an unmade bunk against the wall; one rocking chair; and a table. There was a fire burning, and on the hearthstones lay Blitzen. He rose and wagged his tail.

"Hello, boy, hello. Where is your master? Where is that other person?" She hugged his warm chest, smelling that pungent, comforting dog smell. At least there was something else alive in this house besides her.

She walked across the room to another doorway and looked in—a gray, dark kitchen. An ancient cookstove with rusted lids stood in the corner, and the ceiling was hung with supplies: baskets of potatoes, cured hams, bunches of dried herbs. Sacks of beans and coffee and a barrel of flour were under the table. Wind rattled the window, and the lace curtains blew straight out. She bet *Ada* had made those curtains—decorative and useless.

"Hello? Hello?" Sarah flapped her arms and went back to the main room. She peered out the window. Nothing but white, and sometimes flecks of gray swirling and whirling. She

63

was alone. All she could hear was the swish of the snow. She looked at Alex's library. Hawthorne. Melville and Scott. Tennyson's poems. A phrenology book. She felt the shape of her skull beneath her hair. The different bumps and hollows probably showed her to be headstrong and grumpy. There was a guide to wildflowers and a book of home remedies. Sarah sighed and wandered over to the rocking chair by the fire. A depressing green willow was embroidered on the headrest. Ada's handiwork, she was sure. It made her feel quite pulled down. Sarah sat carefully. The storm scoured the roof of the cabin, and breezes pushed at the hem of her skirt. She tucked her hands inside her jacket and squeezed her face up to keep from crying. I am a mail-order bride. I have been sent, received, and *deceived*, but there is no one here! They've all gone—wherever they go, out here in this godforsaken place. Goody was right. I didn't know what I was getting myself into. Mary was wrong. He's not a fine fellow. He's abandoned me. And that person who soaked my feet last night is gone, too.

Her neck prickled, and she wanted to howl like a wolf. Sarah jumped up, hurried into the kitchen, and found a tin coffeepot on the stove. She poured the brew into a cup and sipped it—barely warm. She shivered and stared bleakly out the window, not hungry. The mountains were hidden by the snow. Sarah flapped her arms and loaded wood into the firebox. The heat only pushed at the cold, like weak fingers. Maybe they've all gone away—I'll be on my own in this gray, freezing house forever. Then the kitchen door opened. Snow gusted in on a bitter wind, with something small and bundled.

"Whooh! Cold!" The door slammed and the snow blew across the floor. "Hi—you like it cold? You not delicate flower

64

like other one. Whooh, cold!" The short person whirled across the room, flung off a shapeless garment, and hovered by the stove. "Fingers! Watch out for these." He held up a blackened forefinger. "They go first. I say to Mr. Proud, no, no eggs today—too cold. But he say, Chang? You get eggs for Mrs. Proud. She need building up, he say." He stared at her, and she stared back; he wore a padded coat and hat, and had a long pigtail down his back. He was the first Chinese she had ever seen. Then Sarah smiled, glad to see anyone who was alive.

"I not need building up—I mean, I don't need building up."

"That's what I say. But Mr. Proud? When he want something, you go do. So—here are eggs." He dumped them into a black frying pan on the stove. They landed with a thud.

Sarah touched them. They were frozen. "What do I *do* with them?"

"Don't know. You decide. We eat breakfast long ago. Time clean up now." He bustled about the kitchen, taking up more room than he needed, Sarah thought; heating water on the stove, getting out his scrub brush, sweeping the floor with sharp jabs.

Sarah stared at the eggs, then put them in a pan near the oven to unfreeze.

"Old oven, Mr. Chang." She snapped the door shut.

"Not old." Snow flew before his broom. "Well used, like grandfather."

"Like a dying grandfather! You should get a new one. 'Course, I've heard everything's so expensive out West."

Chang nodded vigorously. "Too much money. Mr. Proud not like spend money."

Sarah wondered if that was so. Hadn't he sent money for her trip? "Isn't it hard to cook for everyone on this stove?"

"No." He rested his chin on the broom. "Chang used to it. Chang do *all* cooking."

"Well, now that I'm here, I can help. Mr. Proud did advertise for someone who could cook."

"Don't need help. Chang do all by himself. Lady eat, lady knit, lady sew, but lady not cook."

Sarah clattered the pot on the stove. "We'll see about that."

They stared at each other across the stove. Chang folded his arms into his sleeves and stood straighter and taller. Sarah buttoned her top button and held her head higher.

A sudden thought struck her, and she couldn't help asking, "Were you—did you—put me to bed last night?" Had this man seen her *skin?*

He laughed, tiny, soft laughs. "You were *very* sleepy, lady. Eyes fall down, mouth fall open—I take care of you."

The thought of being undressed by Chang appalled her. What would Goody say? What would Cissy say? My Lord, even Dan Monroe who kisses like a horse begins to look good from here.

"I don't need taking care of." Sarah gulped her coffee and choked.

"No, no. Lady not need taking care of." He thumped her hard on the back and chuckled.

The front door banged and Sarah saw Alex enter the living room, snow drifting from his shoulders and hat. He seemed immense, and Sarah shrank back, feeling stiff and small. His arms were at an awkward angle, and at first, she thought he'd brought in a bundle of snow.

66

"Mrs. Proud, come here." He hurried to the fireplace and knelt down. Unfolding his arms, he set down a white shape on the warm hearthstones and shrugged off his coat and hat. "Blankets, please. Ask Chang—he knows where they are."

Sarah followed Chang up the steps to his loft. He opened a cupboard at the head of the stairs and handed her a worn blanket. Sarah ran downstairs and saw Alex kneeling on the hearthstones, stroking the head of a gray sheep.

"What's wrong with her?" Sarah crouched beside him and tucked the blanket around the ewe. She rubbed its coat and smelled the rich, oily smell of lamb's wool. It reminded her of home, and suddenly she didn't feel quite so small.

"I don't know." Alex sighed. "Call me a fool for bringing her in, but I couldn't leave her in the barn—it's too cold for her. She was the first good breeder I bought years ago." He stroked the sheep's ears and wiped her nose with the edge of the blanket.

Sarah went into the kitchen, calling over her shoulder, "I'm going to heat up some water, oats, and molasses. It's what I always gave to our sick sheep."

"Good idea, Mrs.—Sarah."

She hurried to fill a saucepan, threw in some oats, gouged out thick molasses from a crock, and set it on the stove. Though she stood next to it, the heat barely warmed her. She took sticks from the woodbox and fed the fire. When the water finally bubbled, she poured it into a bowl and brought it out to the main room. Dipping a rag in, she opened the ewe's mouth and squeezed the liquid inside. The sheep coughed.

"Give her more," Alex said.

Sarah dipped and squeezed, and she forgot herself and the marriage, watching the old sheep. "Come on," she whispered. "Swallow." The liquid and oats dribbled out of its mouth. Quickly, Sarah rubbed the chest and belly of the ewe. It coughed again, and its pink tongue moved.

Sarah chuckled. "It will get better. Poor thing, out in that terrible cold. No wonder it got sick." She stroked its ears, and the warmth from the animal passed into Sarah and soothed her. The ewe raised its head briefly and sighed.

"It will get well, Alex, I know it will."

He smiled at her over the sheep and nodded. "You did say in your letter you were gentle with animals—Sarah."

Yes, I am gentle with animals, she thought. But not always with people. The memory of the wedding and the frozen ride across the prairie came back to her, and she clenched her fingers into the sheep's wool.

CHAPTER NINE

"And then was Mercy White," Chang said, over the clatter of stove lids that noon. "She plant corn last June and blizzard come up. She not know any better—greenhorn"— he glanced at Sarah making coffee—"and not get in house at once. Mr. Proud found her week later, curled up on prairie." Chang tucked his hands under his face like a sleeping child. "She never wake up."

Sarah banged the pot onto the stove and sliced salt pork up to fry.

"Then," Chang went on, sweeping the floor with a frazzled broom, "was John Bascombe. Came on train to be rancher last fall. Leave depot when storm in west. Any fool see cloud on horizon. It take months to find him—under dead tree, try find shelter. Greenhorns!" He pushed the dirt into an ancient pan and dumped it in a pail.

"Well, it's not their fault they don't know what to do."

Chang straightened the tablecloth. "Maybe—maybe not. Greenhorns should stay home. Montana not place for know-nothings."

Sarah glared at Chang. He was deliberately goading her, making her feel a useless stranger.

"I'm sure you were new one time yourself, Mr. Chang." The words were tight and thin in her mouth. She was trying to be polite, trying not to make enemies as soon as she arrived. She stabbed at the salt pork.

69

"I never new," he chuckled, "never. I always old."

Sarah lifted her head higher and took the food out to the table set up by the fire. Now she would meet the hired hands, Alex had said. The ewe was still sleeping on the hearth, fenced in by three chairs.

The door opened and slammed, opened and slammed as the hands came in and shed their coats. They all seemed the same to Sarah: brown, wiry men in worn flannel shirts, denim pants, and red neckcloths. All three had beards and assorted stained teeth.

"Howdy, I'm William. Welcome, ma'am," said one, and lowered himself into a seat. He had more hair than the others.

"Fred," mumbled another as he sat. He was lanky, with big wrists. "Chang? This good stuff this time? None of that hishy-hashy stew?"

Chang glared at him as the last hand said, "Don't make him angry, Fred. Admit that his fried eggs are good. I'm Jake." He held out his hand and shook Sarah's. "Glad to have you here. This place needs a woman. We need a woman before we turn into desperadoes who forget how to shave and only swear and spit." He sat down at the table.

Sarah smiled at his round, weathered face. She was appreciated—welcome! Chang set down a plate of browned potatoes, biscuits, and salt pork. Sarah brought in the pot of coffee and poured it out.

"Ah," Alex rubbed his hands. "That's good—a woman pouring out coffee. That warms the heart."

She glanced at him warily. Pa never said anything like that.

"Here, come sit by me, Mrs.—Sarah." Her husband

pulled out a chair and settled her in, gently. Never in her whole life had anyone held out a chair for her.

Alex bowed his head. "For what we are about to receive, let us give thanks."

The men mumbled and then set to on the food. Sarah had never seen people eat so fast or so silently. All she could hear was the wind whining outside, the hiss of snow against the walls, and men chewing and swallowing. She looked quickly at Alex. He didn't seem quite so old as the first time she saw him. Was he fifty? Sixty? His skin was firm, if wrinkled, eyes bright, and she could see no hairs in his ears. Pa had tufts in his.

"Chilly today," Sarah said, trying to fill up the cold spaces.

"Mmmph. Not so's you'd notice," said Fred.

"Is it always this cold the end of April?" Sarah asked.

"Always? What's always?" Jake said. "Out West there are only sometimes and todays and tomorrows. Just as you think you've got it figured out, the weather changes. Sun dries up the water holes. Winter freezes half of your cattle. Indians and rustlers make off with the rest. Never get bored here." He chuckled.

"Do the Indians bother your ranch, Mr. Proud?" she said.

He set down his fork and wiped his moustache. "Not often. Sometimes the young men send out a raiding party and take a few horses or cattle. I tell you, though, the white men are more trouble than the Indians."

"Not true, boss," Fred said.

"Who took twenty cattle last spring, Fred?" Alex said.

"Mmmph."

71

"Who disappeared into the badlands and we couldn't even follow them?"

"What United States Cavalry made stupid, blundering mistakes?" Jake broke in. "Never get your cattle back for you, never—and rules? God—excuse me, ma'am—gosh, their rules are enough to drive you crazy."

"What kind of rules?" Sarah finished her meal and set her fork and knife neatly in the middle of her plate.

"Well, for instance—if some Indians *do* make off with your horses, and the cavalry don't get lost and catches 'em—then the army follows the braves to the reservation and watches the horses get put in with the Indians' herd. Good-bye horses. Never see 'em again. That's the rules."

"Why, that's just plain silly." Sarah was indignant. "They're your horses—you work them and feed them—I wonder if Mary Burkett knows about that."

"Who is Mary Burkett?" her husband asked.

"Oh, just a friend I met on the train. She's stationed with her husband at Fort Custer."

"Maybe we could go there sometime in the summer, to see your friend. Would you like that?" He smiled at her.

It was tempting—a husband who wanted to give you treats. But she had been deceived. No treat could make up for that. "Perhaps," she said coldly. "Perhaps."

"Well, ma'am." Jake pushed back his chair. "Thank you for the fine food, and we are glad you're here. You do brighten up the place. Why, I haven't seen a woman since that dance in town in February."

"That wasn't a woman, Jake," Fred said. "That was Mabel Star—she ain't no woman."

"Shh," Alex said. "That's enough, boys. Ladies are present."

Mabel Star—who was she? If she wasn't a woman, what was she?

Alex cleared his throat and rose. "I'll be in the barn, Mrs.—Sarah, if you need anything. Chang, here, will take care of you." The others scraped their chairs back and left the house, boots thumping out the door.

The kitchen felt like a Maine lake, and Sarah pulled the table closer to the stove. She got out her inkwell and pen, breathing on her hands to warm them. Chang gave one disapproving glance and began to wash the dishes.

"Dear Goody," she began. The pen sputtered and the ink slowed to a black sludge. "Drat!" Sarah jumped up and put the inkwell on the stove. A minute later she dipped her pen in, sat, and wrote rapidly.

"You would hardly credit how good-tempered and busy I have been since I arrived yesterday. All we have had is blizzard and wind. I am beginning to hate the sight of snow." No sense in telling her Chang's awful stories.

"Mr. Proud is a bit older than I thought, than we thought." Sarah went to the stove, grabbed the warm inkwell, and took it back to the table. She wanted to write, "Mr. Proud is ancient, ancient. And Mr. Chang is more Chinese than I thought. And I am lonelier than I thought. And it is colder and bleaker than I thought, and I haven't even seen the mountains yet that were part of the whole trip." She put a hand over her heart; it felt bruised.

A drop fell on the paper and blurred "Dear." Sarah wiped her eyes hastily. She would not let that man with the pigtail

73

see her crying—greenhorn tears, he'd probably call them. He washed the dishes with loud *clinks*.

"The house is a good size, Aunt, with a big main room, a loft overhead, and a bedroom and kitchen. The three hands, all nice men, live in a separate cabin. Mr. Proud is kind." That was true—that would comfort Goody. "Also, there is a Chinese cook." That would really cheer her aunt. "It is so cold, the eggs are frozen and I have to warm my ink on the stove. There is not much else to say. I just arrived and wanted you to know I am well and safe. Soon I will know more and will write again. Your loving niece, Sarah."

She pushed back her chair and stared at the white window, ignoring Chang.

That night, Chang's slippers slapped up the stairs to his loft, *slap-thump, slap-thump*. Sarah watched him go and wished he would stay. Now she would be alone with Alex. Now they would do whatever married people did, unless he was too old. Maybe, she sighed, maybe he was too old for a honeymoon night. Maybe they could be partners, sort of like a brother and sister, running the ranch together—

"Sarah." She looked up. He stood by her, holding out his hand. "Come. We are well rested, your journey is done, and . . ." He nodded. It was clear what he meant: "It is time for our wedding night."

Nervously, she followed him into their bedroom, though she'd already come to think of it as *her* bedroom. The wind scraped and hissed against the walls.

He took off his wool shirt and vest and hung them on a peg. "Chilly, isn't it." His voice sounded thin in the cold air.

"Oh, yes," Sarah chattered, "yes, indeed." She took that

74

as a handy excuse and jumped fully dressed into bed. Sarah wondered what would happen if she didn't undress. Would he laugh at her? Goody would trot out a homily, as usual: "You've made your bed, now lie in it." What could she do? She didn't know if she wanted to leave. And how could she put him off for weeks and weeks? Clumsily, fumbling with the buttons, Sarah pulled her clothes off under the covers. She felt even smaller, reduced to a child in her underwear.

"Here, Mrs. Proud—Sarah—I'll take those." He stood by the bed and took her waist, skirt, and petticoat, one by one. Like a child carrying an egg in a spoon, he relayed the garments to pegs on the wall. It was strange to see him touching her clothes, too private, as if part of herself had been hung on the wall. She felt queer and did not know where to look. She didn't mean to watch him, but out of the corner of her eye she saw him touch the petticoat to his cheek. Then he took off his thick wool pants and shirt, revealing a union suit, and slid in under the covers.

Sarah moved away to her edge of the bed. "Where did you find Mr. Chang?" she babbled.

"Chang?" Alex rubbed his moustache. "He used to cook for a hotel in the town next to us. There was some trouble. . . ."

"What kind of trouble?"

"Over a horse. Someone accused him of stealing one, and they were ready to ride him out of town, or worse—but I stopped them."

"How?" Keep talking, she thought, keep talking.

He grinned. "Told them I'd beat their brains in if they hurt him, that he was *my* cook, hired that day, and they'd have to fight *me* if they hurt him."

75

"And they let him go?" What kind of man had she married? A vigilante who took the law into his own hands?

"Of course. And I gave them one of my horses to make up for the one they'd lost. 'Course Chang didn't take it—he *hates* horses—and he came back and has been here ever since."

"Oh." Sarah couldn't think of anything else to say.

"Are you happy here, Mrs.—Sarah?" he asked.

His leg bumped hers, and she drew it back quickly. The wind rattled the windows; somewhere a mouse squeaked, and a log settled in the fire.

"Happy?" Sarah finally said. "What is happy? Can you ride it? No! Can you eat it? No! Then, Lord, what *good* is it?"

After a startled moment, he laughed. "I take it, then, that you are not happy, Mrs.—Sarah."

She rose on one elbow, all her anger coming back when she thought of her hopes and dreams around the tall, lithe man on a Western horse. "I thought you'd be younger. Your picture showed a younger man. You deceived me!"

He cleared his throat. "I know, it was a deception. But if I'd sent a recent picture, you'd never have come. And I'm as good as a young man any day." He sat up and slapped his chest. "I'm only sixty—I've got twenty good years left. I can ride with the young men, rope steers, stay all day in the rain and never catch cold, *and* dance all night."

He pulled her close and kissed her cheek. Sarah pushed him away and burst into tears. He's too big—too loud—and I'm too young! Oh, I wish I'd never left home—I wish Goody were here right now this minute—she'd know what to do. What if he kisses me again? At least it isn't like kissing a horse— like Cissy's Dan Monroe. Oh, Jesus, God, protect me, I'm so small. She hiccoughed and Alex offered her the sleeve of his union suit. She wiped her eyes and nose, and he patted her hand. "There, there, Sary, don't worry. There, there."

"My name is Sarah," she sniffed. "You don't know me well enough—to call me Sary."

CHAPTER TEN

She woke to silence and an empty bed. Thank goodness he was gone. It was like going to sleep with a sore throat, forgetting it during the night, and then remembering as soon as you opened your mouth in the morning. Last night. Their first together as man and wife. Sarah turned and pulled the covers over her ears. Mary was right. What happens between a man and woman isn't something you can explain to another. She wondered if it would be different if he were younger. Could it be like learning to ride a horse? The first time was horrible. And frightening. The next time you still caught your breath, but it wasn't so bad?

She wished she could write a letter to Mary—a letter where she could say what she truly felt.

Dear Mary, she imagined writing. *Remember the talk we had at Mrs. Laynor's Lodgings? When you said, "You'll have to find out for yourself"? I found out. Husbands keep their union suits on when they take their wives. The buttons hurt. It is very quick—but not quick enough.*

Sarah pressed her cold hands together, remembering. At first, she was afraid she'd laugh. Then afraid she'd cry. Then she felt suffocated and panicky when he lowered himself over her. Sarah thought he hummed a little. Then sighed. And she lay flat and helpless on the bed, the tears rolling down her cheeks. Something that was hers—that she didn't even *know* was hers—had been taken. And when it was done, he turned over, patted her hand, and said, "I hope for children."

Sarah sighed. He hoped—what about her? But she couldn't lie in bed all day, brooding. That's probably what Ada would have done. Sarah Adams Goodhue would get up and go on with things as if nothing had happened. She would push all thoughts of last night into a tiny room inside and close the door.

Outside the wind had stopped, and the sun blazed on a sparkling white land. Squares of yellow lay across the blanket, and Sarah put her hand in one and felt little warmth. It was May 1. She examined her hand. It looked the same. Nothing on it would say, "This is the hand of a married woman." Could people tell? When she sat at the supper table with Jake and all the rest, would they know, somehow? The problem with the tiny room was, the door kept opening and thoughts sneaked out.

She pulled her clothes under the covers to warm them, wriggled into a skirt, waist, and sweater, and finished dressing outside the covers. It was so cold that she pulled on a pair of thick gloves. Chang was singing in the kitchen, a high, tuneless song that descended and merged with the clatter of pans. Chang. Today was the day to assert her place here. If she had to bear the trials of a wife, at least she could run the house.

She listened, shivering in the bitter cold. No other sound. Alex was gone. She threw a thick shawl around her shoulders, crossed and belted it at her waist. Good. Maybe she wouldn't have to face him until tonight, and then she could look at him without reddening. She left her room slowly, looking out to see if anyone was there. The sheep was gone from the hearthstones, and Blitzen was not to be seen. She missed his comforting face.

The pans clattered again, and Sarah hesitated before joining Chang in the kitchen.

"Hello, lady." He stirred a large pot of oatmeal on the stove. He had on his thickest padded coat and also wore gloves. He shivered as he stirred.

"Morning, Chang. Is Alex—outside? Where's the sick sheep?"

"*Mr. Proud,*" he emphasized the words, "in barn, with sick cow. He took sheep with him. Others clear path."

She hurried to fill the coffeepot. "Cold today, Chang. Can't we build up that fire more?"

He shook his head. "Stove old. Heat come out and—poof!" He waved his fingers in the air.

Sarah set the pot on the stove top to boil. Keep busy. Behave as always, and no one will know about last night. "They'll be hungry this morning. Bacon," she muttered, and unstrung the ham from the rafter. Her hands fumbled, and she almost dropped the meat.

Chang smiled and patted his hat. "Sleep well, lady?"

"Of course, Mr. Chang." Sarah sawed at the ham. "I *always* sleep well." Drat the man. Drat his insinuations.

Then he frowned and laid down his spoon. "Lady, no bacon with oatmeal."

"Why ever not?" Sarah stopped, midway through an uneven slice.

"He say wasteful." Chang gave the oatmeal a ferocious stir.

"Oh, he does?" Sarah continued slicing and laid the pink-and-white slabs in a black iron pan. The thick slices comforted her.

80

"Tcch." Chang made as if to take the pan off, but Sarah put out her hand.

"That's enough! I say we will have bacon, and by God, we will have bacon!" Sarah stabbed at the slices, turning them far too frequently. The fat sizzled and hissed and made her feel better.

"*And* I think I'll make cornmeal cakes, too."

"Lady!" Chang stood in shocked silence.

Sarah felt as if a small fire burned in her chest and with each new, daring action, it burned brighter and hotter.

She threw handfuls of cornmeal from the sack into a blue mixing bowl, heated some frozen milk in a pan, and began to mix it. "And an egg." She reached for the last one in a basket beside the stove, cracked it against the side of the bowl, and heard a dull sound. She peeled back the shell and saw frozen egg white.

"This is ridiculous, Chang. Frozen eggs by the stove. We'll have to get a new one. Lord, it never got this cold in Maine."

Chang set his mouth in a thin line and hummed a grating tune.

Sarah, the fire burning hotter inside, sang loudly. "Old Dan Tucker, it's too late to get your supper. . . ."

They would have bacon and oatmeal and coffee and corn cakes, and damn Chang's stinginess. If she had to bear the trials of a wife, at least she could eat well.

She didn't hear Alex when he entered the kitchen, she singing loudly and turning the corn cakes, Chang refusing to give up his position by the stove and almost shrieking his tune.

"Good Lord, what—is—going on here?" Alex bellowed.

Sarah stopped singing but did not turn around. Chang pursed his lips and muttered, "Bacon, Mr. Proud, bacon *with* oatmeal."

"*And* corn cakes," Sarah sang.

After a moment's silence, Alex nodded. "Just what we need on a morning like this." He did not look at Sarah when he spoke.

Sarah lifted her nose at Chang, flung the corn cakes on a plate, and hurried into the main room. The table was drawn up next to the fireplace, where the logs sputtered and flared. Blitzen was already curled in his favorite place, snoring.

Jake sat down and rubbed his hands. "Corn cakes! My very favorite."

Quickly, Sarah put out the smoking bacon and hot coffee as Chang set the oatmeal in the center of the table.

There was a hushed silence about the table, as in church during prayer, until the food was gone. As Sarah watched them eat, she realized no one knew (except Chang) or even cared about last night. There were more important things on their minds than her first night as a married woman.

Jake rose, bowed in her direction, and said, "As far as I'm concerned, ma'am, the gods smiled on Mr. Proud when you came West."

Fred muttered, "Can't you talk normal, Jake? Not like somebody that ate a book for breakfast?" He paused. "We sure are lucky."

William smiled shyly and bobbed his head, and Sarah felt the fire inside soothe down to a glowing coal. She was appreciated! Here was something to warm the heart.

Alex pushed back his chair and said, "I agree with them all—we *are* lucky. I'm going into town today—maybe there's a letter from home, Sarah, or from your friend."

She looked up. That was kind of him—a letter from home. There might be one, if Goody had written just after she'd left to go West. To see Goody's crabbed handwriting, to hear news of the farm, of Cissy—it made her eyes water, and she wiped them hastily.

"I'll go with you," Jake offered.

"Then the rest of you should work in the barn today," Alex said. "Keep an eye on the sick animals and grease all the harnesses." Fred groaned.

Sarah rose and dabbed at her mouth. "Is it safe—Alex?" She did not look at him. "Couldn't the storm come up again?" If he were lost in a blizzard, if he died—what would happen to her? Left on her own with Chang and their battles in the middle of nowhere?

"Oh, it's safe enough—that storm's worn out by now." Alex disappeared into the other room and returned carrying his bearskin coat and hat. "If we worried about *safe* all the time, we wouldn't be here."

"That's right," Jake said. "We'd be back East dressed in some kind of mummified outfit, prancing off to work each day." He minced across the floor and then began to swagger. "This is how we walk out West—real men." He thumped his chest, and Sarah laughed.

"We'll be back before nighttime. Don't worry: Chang and Blitzen will take care of you." Alex glanced at her shyly, wrestled into his coat and hat, and was gone.

"Well." Sarah rubbed her hands together. "Well, then." She watched Chang ferrying dishes to the kitchen. *He* knew what to do. *Fred* knew what to do, as did Alex and William and Jake. The dog knew his job was to sleep and guard the

83

cabin. Only *she* did not know what to do. Back home Sarah had seen a railroad car derailed—they'd all ridden out to see it. She felt that way now—off track, stranded, and useless. She wandered into the kitchen as Chang poured steaming water into an enameled pan and began to wash dishes. That was it. Goody always said, "When you don't know what to do, wash something."

Sarah tightened her shawl. "I think I'll turn out the kitchen today, Mr. Chang."

"Turn out?" he repeated.

"Clean. Scrub. Make clean for Mr. Proud." She caught herself, realizing she was speaking broken English.

Chang grunted and filled a large pot on the stove. One by one, like a doctor laying out instruments for an operation, he placed on the table one worn brush, a cake of yellow soap, two torn gray rags, and a rusted basin.

Sarah gazed at these, and the glowing coal inside flared again. "No mop, Chang?"

He shook his head.

"No broom?"

He grinned and gestured at a balding tool in the corner.

Sarah rolled up her sleeves, shrieked at the cold, and rolled them down again. She noticed that Chang's wash water had stopped steaming and that he moved his hands quickly in and out of the pan. Cold already? She pushed at the floor with the tattered broom, and watched the dirt escape through the sparse bristles. Work—work was the answer. Keep busy. Fill up the spaces with words and work, then that door won't open and let the thought sneak out: You-have-been-un-wrapped-and-you-didn't-like-it.

When the floor was swept clean, Chang picked up the

pan of old dishwater and started toward the door. His hand slipped, the pan clattered to the floor, and water splashed out in a widening pool.

He jumped back, as did Sarah, and she saw the quick fear in his eyes. He clenched and unclenched his right hand.

"Stiff, lady, cold fingers. Don't tell Mr. Proud."

Sarah put out her hand. "It's all right, Mr. Chang. Don't worry. I'd planned on washing the floor, anyway." She swept the water out across the boards and splashed a long stream onto the floor from the teakettle. She was enjoying this.

Chang picked up the brush and knelt to scrub, but Sarah stopped him. "No, wait, Chang. Let it soak in. It needs to get *really* wet to get clean."

He raised his eyebrows at her and rose stiffly. "I go work in next room, then. Too wet for me here."

Sarah tiptoed through the water and opened the kitchen door to empty her dustpan. And gasped. In all her worry and busyness, she had forgotten to look. The white land rolled away, past the brown smudge of the barn, past the gray corral and a few jack pines. The mountains rose, sudden, abrupt, and so blue that her eyes teared. The mountains filled her eyes, the inside of her head, until Sarah felt that intense blue was in her from her hair down to her toes. She shivered and pulled her shawl closer.

Ma was wrong. Mountains don't just lift up the heart: They lift the hair on the back of the neck. They fill the eyes and make the heart pound. *This* is what you have married— not a man, but a land. A cold, blue, windy land. Sarah breathed in the crisp, new air and thought: Don't leave yet. Give this a chance. She looked at the mountains. I will wait until the geese fly in the fall and then—if I can't bear it anymore—then I'll leave. Besides, as Pa would say, what was happy? Could you eat it? No! Could you ride it? No! Then, Lord, what *good* was it?

"Lady, close door! Are you crazy?" Chang rushed in from the other room and slammed it shut. He went back to the stove and held out his hands, muttering, the sounds clicking and hissing. Sarah wondered if they were ancient Chinese curses.

Then he tapped his foot on the floor. It made a dull sound. "Oh, lady!" He knelt and tapped the floor with his finger. It made a clicking sound.

"Oh, Chang." Sarah stared at what had once been a wet floor, and now was an ice-covered space. Frozen eggs were one thing. Freezing sheets and clothes and wearing gloves inside the house were another. But ice in the kitchen! The small pond went from the door to the window.

Then Sarah began to laugh. She stepped into the main room and ran in, skidding across to the kitchen door. Blitzen ran beside her, barking and leaping. "Down, boy." She turned and slid back.

"Come on, Chang. Skate with me." She held out her hands.

He stared at her and folded his arms into his sleeves. "No, lady—not funny." He frowned at her and tiptoed over the ice out to the main room of the house. But, almost in spite of himself, he watched as Sarah slid and flew, twirled and dipped, and the dog barked.

"Backwards! Look, Chang, I can still skate backwards." She was a child again on a frozen lake in Maine, trying to master the difficult art: "How, Pa, how?" And he'd shrugged his shoulders and skated backwards, easily.

Chang gave her a horrified look. She said loudly, "I'd've brought my skates if I'd known there would be an indoor rink."

Old thing, disapproving old thing! He was as bad as the schoolmarm back home. And, just for effect, she did an elaborate twirl before she stopped.

"My." Sarah held a hand to her chest. "I guess I'm warm enough now."

The afternoon became darker and more bitter as the sun disappeared behind a bank of clouds. Though Chang fed the fire regularly, the ice did not melt. Sarah sat on the bunk in the main room with Blitzen curled at her feet and tried to read a book of home remedies. There was no remedy for loneliness—for deception. The authors seemed to care only about healing ague and weak chests. Sarah patted hers and looked out the window again. The land was white, and white blew across it. The windowpanes shook and rattled, and she worried. What if a storm came up? What if Alex didn't come back?

Finally, as the sun set over the mountains in a blaze of red and violet, Sarah saw the horses and sled pulling into the yard. The two men jumped down, handed the reins to Fred, and stomped into the house.

"My!" Jake said, unwrapping his stiff muffler. "Good to be back. It's bitter out there." Blitzen sniffed his trouser legs and wagged vigorously.

Alex handed her a packet of letters, and Sarah seized on them. "Thank you!" She recognized Goody's writing on one, and what might be Mary's writing on another. She pocketed them to read later on.

"Are you all right?" She took Alex's coat and shook the snow off. "How are your hands?"

He grinned and flexed them. "They'll do."

"How was your second day here, Mrs.—Sarah?"

She felt stiff, shy. "All right—all right."

"Hey," Jake said, "what's the matter with Chang?"

Alex turned and watched his cook tiptoeing about the kitchen, arms outstretched for balance. They went to the doorway and Alex said, "Chang? What's wrong?"

The cook turned slowly and opened his mouth, but Sarah cut in. "It was *my* fault, Alex. I was washing the floor and I left the door open too long."

Chang gave her a long look and then patted his hat.

Alex frowned. "You have to be careful, Sary. . . ."

She tapped her foot. "Sarah. If we had a newer stove, this wouldn't have happened."

They stayed fixed for a moment—Chang, Alex, and Sarah—until Jake began to laugh and held out his hands.

"May I, Mrs. Proud?"

He seized her arms and skated across the floor, turned and whizzed back again. Humming a marching tune, Jake twirled her around and flew past the two astonished men. Chang seized the dog's collar and held on tightly.

Sarah began to laugh, sputtering and hooting. Here was someone after her own heart. Merry! Not old, at the end of his life. Not old, with white hair and bushy eyebrows. Then she felt a strong tap on her shoulder. Alex cut in and skated her around faster and faster, with fancy dips and swings.

Breathless and panting, they stopped and Sarah pushed back her hair.

Alex said, "I didn't tell you about that in the advertisement, did I?"

"Tell me what?"

"That Mr. Proud's ranch has an indoor skating rink."

Jake laughed.

"I guess if I'd put that in, some belle from New York would've come here." Alex gave Sarah an appraising glance. She straightened her skirts and patted her hair. What was wrong? This was it—he wished he'd gotten someone else. Someone pretty and accomplished. Maybe even tall.

He reached out and tweaked her nose. "Yep, some nice belle instead of this little dab of a person."

"Dabs are as good as belles any day," Sarah snapped.

" 'Course they are." He picked her up, swung her around, and planted her on the ice. "*And* they make the best skating partners."

CHAPTER ELEVEN

The next week was the same as the days back home in Dewborne, yet not the same. Sarah sat at the kitchen table, trying to read and stay warm. Carlyle's pamphlets. Solid, dull stuff. The kind of thing Mrs. Owens from the train would like. Pure thinking and clean living. Sarah didn't know about pure thinking, but she surely couldn't get any cleaner. Up in the morning to make breakfast with the wind scouring the cabin walls. Struggle with that dratted stove while Chang looked on and smiled. Then washing up in an old battered pan. Then sweep the kitchen and the living room and their bedroom. Try not to listen to the wind. Make the bed. Try not to think about what happened at night. Though, thankfully, it didn't seem to happen too often. Sarah wondered how often you had to do it to have children. No one had told her anything. She didn't even know if she wanted children, much less to be married. Married—to a man old enough to be her grandfather, to a Chinese cook who enjoyed watching her fumble, to three hired hands who all looked the same, and to a land. Here, Sarah smiled. And to a land. She watched a crow rowing its way from one tall pine to another, protesting against the cold. And the sky was like a river that went on forever—clean, fresh, new.

Sarah flipped a page and wondered if Alex and the hands were all right. He'd taken them out to check on the beeves, to see how they were surviving the cold. They'd spread some hay out beyond the corral, hoping the weaker cows would come in and feed. She'd done all her chores; the bread was rising on the warming rack, as much as it could in this evil cold; and though she'd mending to do, she was putting it off. She could hear Blitzen snoring by the fire.

For a brief moment, Sarah wondered about a child. "This is your father, sweetheart." Pointing to Alex, with his white hair and bushy white eyebrows. "This is your family—Chang, Jake, William, and Fred. We are all happy here. Or a little bit like happy, only different." She'd not be able to lie to a child. It was one thing to stay stiff and silent in bed at night, hoping, hoping. And trying not to pull away too much. She didn't know why she cared about Alex's feelings. She shouldn't, not after what he'd done—deceived and tricked her.

"Oh, fuss," she heard Goody's words in her mind. "We're not rich, she ain't good-lookin', and she's wild and undisciplined."

If she hadn't married Alex, who would have married her? Who? Wasn't this better than "drying up like an old rooster," as Goody said?

The light lengthened and the dark crept in like black dye—flowing from the mountains, down to the prairie, dark, dark, up to the house, and sweeping over it. Sarah shivered and stood up. She was getting spooky. If she didn't watch out, she'd end up like Hannah Turner, walking into the sea with her hat on.

Sarah threw her shawl around her shoulders and put on her cape and mittens. "Chicken," she said out loud. "I shall amaze them with my cooking. I will not be depressed. I will not be downtrodden. I will eat!" She marched outside into the dark and the fierce wind.

91

Holding a shawl tight against her stinging cheeks, she followed the cabin's wall to the first shed, where the chickens were. She pulled open the door against the wind and swept in. The chickens hardly moved. In the dusk, she could just see their huddled, inky forms all bunched together for warmth. "Oh, Lord, it's cold." That's what Cissy always said: "Oh, Lord." She reached out and then saw a small blot against the straw. Funny shape—stiff and—"Frozen!" Sarah picked it up and shook it. "Don't be dead, little clucky, don't be dead." It was stupid, seeing as she would twist its neck in a moment. But it didn't seem fair, somehow, to have it already be dead. She shook it again. Definitely dead. A chicken who had seen better days. She started to giggle, and then stopped. What kind of country was this, where your chickens froze to death in a shed?

Outside, push the door against the wind, then slam it shut, tight. Maybe the other hens would be all right. Then through the wind, keeping one gloved hand on the rough wall, to the safe yellow square of the kitchen door.

Bang. Inside, Chang was building up the fire, and she could hear Alex humming in the next room, back from his ride to check the cattle.

She held out the frozen bird to Chang. "Look!"

"Mmm?" He jammed wood into the cookstove.

"Look!"

He stared at the chicken and then chuckled. "So, it easier than wringing neck. I hate wringing neck. That little sound they make."

"But it's so cold. What about the others, Chang? Shouldn't we bring them in by the stove?"

"Mmm. Yes. I go get them in big basket. You leave chicken for me."

"Oh, no." She took off her shawl and cloak. "*I'm* going to cook tonight." She went over to the stove and picked up the teakettle. Holding the chicken over the washing pan in the sink, she poured steaming water over it, making sure all of its feathers got soaked. Then she swished it around in a panful of hot water. "Come on, little clucky, unfreeze!" She began to pull out the feathers, one by one. They came out reluctantly, with a dull *pop!* at the end. The skin was still partly frozen, and the feet stuck out in a horrible way.

The door banged, and Chang bustled in with two large baskets filled with chickens. "Whooh! Glad you found that dead one, lady. After tonight, no more hens. Jake very sad at no roast chicken. Me, too." He set up a barrier of boards to one side of the stove and let the birds free inside. "I put them back tomorrow if warm enough." The chickens pecked at the floor, hopped about, and then settled down for a snug sleep.

Chang came over and worked quietly beside her, plucking the tail end of the bird. "Ugh. Horrible sound—*pop!*" he imitated. "Must be sinful bird, to die, eh?"

Sarah wondered if he were serious and glanced at him. His eyes twinkled. "Oh, yes, Chang, most definitely a sinful bird. Stole grain from the others, hogged the water pan, didn't keep its feathers clean—I could go on and on."

He laughed. "What do for stuffing, lady?"

"Do we have an onion?"

Chang shook his head.

"Rice?"

Another shake.

"Sage?"

He nodded and took some gray leaves from a hanging bunch of herbs and held them out. In a bowl she crumbled the sage and mixed in dried bread crumbs, a bit of hot water, and a scoop of very hard butter. Then she spooned it into the chicken, trussed it, and set it to bake.

After dinner, which was eaten in a churchlike hush—Sarah could swear Jake had tears in his eyes as he attacked the chicken, potatoes, and gravy—Alex beckoned to Sarah and sat her down in the rocker by the fire.

"Here, sit, Sary. We need something to listen to besides that wind." He went over to his library and took down a volume. It was Tennyson's poems. He sat opposite her and opened the book.

> "On either side the river lie
> Long fields of barley and of rye,
> That clothe the wold and meet the sky;
> And through the field the road runs by
> To many-towered Camelot;"

Sarah listened to the rolling words. Alex read well. His voice was deep and warm—not an old voice, like Mr. Whitaker's in church, that always quavered and broke on the high notes. She listened to the story of the Lady of Shalott and for a time forgot about feeding, washing, and nights.

Alex closed the book and stood up. "I can see you like it. Let's go to bed—maybe you'll dream of Camelot."

Sarah stretched and frowned. "It made me angry. It's beautiful, Alex, but she just lay down and let things happen to her. Floating away in a dream—webs and mirrors and pale faces . . ." She shook herself.

Alex laughed. "You wouldn't let that happen to you?"

"No—would you? I don't believe in curses. We make our own curses, or—our own dreams. No one makes them for us."

"Well." He smiled. "I can see you're not a romantic. Ada loved that poem."

"Ada!" She would, Sarah thought. Then, to change the subject, she asked, "Is Camelot warmer than here?"

"Maybe. I don't know." He grinned. "It *has* been cold, hasn't it. Even for us, even for Montana Territory. I worry about my cattle, Sary."

"Why?"

"Well, there's only so much shelter out there among the gullies and the ravines. We've had to take them hay we cut last summer. They can still get through to the prairie grass, but some of the cows are getting weaker in this cold."

"They can eat grass all winter?" She leaned forward. Now she would learn something about ranching.

"Sure can. The wind blows most of the snow away. They're tough animals, and the prairie grass is full of nourishment. But if you've got ice, or snow that doesn't shift in the wind, or a spring that doesn't come, then—it's trouble."

She saw the worry lines on his face, and somehow they made him look less big and imposing.

"Could you lose a lot, Alex?"

He sat down again and sighed. "Could. It's happened before. I've seen some carcasses out there already—not too many. But if this keeps up?" He slapped his hands on his

95

knees. "Well, you don't want to hear about this. It's not for a lady's ears; Ada always *hated* cow talk."

"Ada!" Sarah said. "I like cows, Alex. I lived on a farm, remember? I like—your ranch."

He lifted his head. "You do?"

"Yes. I like the way the light comes over the prairie in the morning and at night. I like the birds and—sometimes— the wind and, most of all, I like the mountains."

"So do I." He smiled at her.

"My ma liked the mountains."

"She must have been a wise woman, then."

"She was. Died five years back—I think because Pa never talked to her."

He jerked his head up in surprise. "Sary! People don't die—" He began to laugh. "You're teasing me."

"No, I'm not. People die of no talk—just like your beeves die of no food."

He thought for a moment, staring into the fire. "Well, little Sary, are you getting enough food?" He did not look at her.

"Sometimes, Alex," she said quietly. "It's more talk than Pa ever gave me and more than the boys in Dewborne."

"Stupid boys! I don't know how you got to eighteen and never married."

She flushed with pleasure and then frowned. "Because I made trouble—I put gunpowder in the school stove, and molasses on the minister's saddle. And whenever my beaux wanted to give me flowers, I was thinking about running their farms—how many bushels of apples their trees would give. *Not* romantic, Alex."

He hooted. "But, Sary, don't you see? The things that

made you different out East are *just* the things that make you perfect for the West."

"They are?" She looked at him doubtfully and rubbed Blitzen's head.

"Sure." He tweaked her nose and said, "I'm to bed. I'm too sleepy to talk anymore, though, God knows, I appreciate talk."

He stayed in the doorway a second, waiting, but Sarah did not get up. She rocked and looked at the burning wood, thinking of Camelot. She kept her feet planted on the floor and thought that if she stayed by the fire, Alex would be asleep by the time she went to bed.

CHAPTER TWELVE

Sarah unfolded Mary's second letter to read again in the early morning light. Alex slept with his back to her, snoring softly. Even though she'd been here three weeks, she was still unused to the sound. The letter read,

Dear Sarah,

I am sorry your Mr. Proud is not what you expected. Life is full of surprises, Will says.

You will learn to live with him, I am sure of it. I have seen countless girls come and go in my three years as an army wife. I know the frail ones by a certain look: "Don't breathe on me, else I'll fall over." And I know the strong ones. You are a strong one, Sarah.

My heart goes out to you. It is not easy being a woman, but remember: We are bringing civilizing ways to the West. Without us, I truly believe the men would sink back to animals. Remember that, try to keep your spirits up, and take camomile tea to refresh yourself.

Your friend,
Mary

Sarah folded it up and put it on the bedstand. Goody's second letter was longer, covered with her crabbed, strong writing.

Dear Sarah,

I sense the complaint under your words. How old is old? Perhaps old means wise. I always like a dignified man myself. You have made your choice, now you must live with it. Things will get better when the babies come, you'll see. And I will come to visit then—if your pa can live on his own.

At least your Mr. Proud likes to talk, which is more than I can say for your pa. No wonder your ma died young, probably of loneliness.

Cissy got married yesterday. She looked like the cat that ate the cream. I can't see that Dan is much of a catch, he has that big weal on his cheek, but then, all Cissy ever wanted was a house of her own.

Read some good books, keep busy, keep that tongue of yours gentled, and remember your Aunt Goody who loves you as much as ever a mother could.

Love,
Aunt Goody

Sarah wiped her nose. Everyone had advice. Head up. Eyes straight. Don't think—do. She listened to Alex's snores. *Plapph—snorrrk! Plapph—snorrrk!* Did Calamity Jane ever get married—to someone who snored? To someone old enough to be her father? I bet not. And if she *did* make such a mistake, I bet she'd ride off into the sunset on her own.

Sarah turned over and sighed. How could she ride off into the sunset when she didn't have a horse and all it ever did was snow and besides she was so small? She'd been here three weeks, three weeks of snow and wind and silent white days. Though rain and sleet came down just yesterday. And where would she go? Not back home, not to Pa who never talked and Goody who would only fuss and fuss.

"*Slam—rattle—bang!* Sarah sighed again, climbed out of bed, and dressed in the pink light of dawn. *Slam!*

"All right, all right, no need to carry on so," Sarah muttered. Dratted cook. Taking up all that space in the kitchen,

99

announcing his presence so loudly, saying, *Look how useful I am*, all the time.

She scuffed into the kitchen and stared at Chang. He said nothing to her and continued to poke at the stove lids, shake the frying pan, and put more wood into the firebox. She could hear Alex getting up in the far room.

Sarah scuffed back to the fireplace and kicked at the embers. They flew out, and one settled on her boot toe. She watched it burn its way into the leather. A sick animal smell rose, but still she watched.

"Sarah!" Alex grabbed a rag and rubbed out the spark. "What's the matter with you? That's your only pair of boots. You aren't back East, you know, with stores just down the street."

"I know that!" she snapped. "I am out West, the land of opportunity. Home of Calamity Jane." She sat in Ada's chair and vowed not to cry, rocking herself faster and faster.

"You're in a black mood today." Alex disappeared into the kitchen and came back, carrying a mug of coffee. "Here, drink this."

Sarah sipped at the coffee and two tears rolled down her cheeks and splashed onto the front of her jacket. Then another two.

"There, there." With a stiff, outstretched arm, he patted Sarah's head. "What is it, Sary?"

"I'm not Sary—I'm Sarah." She sniffed and wiped her nose on her jacket sleeve. "It's so cold and it's May tenth and there's still snow outside and I haven't seen Calamity Jane yet, and I really wanted to see her—Heroine of Whoop-Up"—she sniffed again—"and my hands are always cold, always, and my feet, too, and cooking on that stove is just impossible."

What she really wanted to do was throw herself on the floor, kick her heels, and wail. But not in front of Alex. Not in front of Chang.

"Well, well. Well. Hmmm. Ada hated the cold, too—"

"I am not Ada! I am young and healthy, but it's time for spring to come."

"I know, I know." He patted her hand heavily. "It's a long way to come for such a little dab of a person, leaving your home behind, a pa and an aunt."

"I'm not a dab." She blew her nose on a handkerchief and stood.

Jake, William, and Fred filed in the front door, heaved their coats on the bunk, and sat at the table. Fred hummed and picked at his teeth. William whittled a piece of wood, while Jake stared at her and whistled. She felt like a mother bird with a nest full of chicks, mouths always open, demanding to be fed. Every morning she would get up and see these same faces. Every morning make coffee in the same darn blue pot. Every morning slice up salt pork and fry it in the same pan.

She went back into the bedroom and splashed water on her face, scrubbing it with a towel. She was too hurried to notice: It was the first morning that the water in the china pitcher was unfrozen.

She sat at the table by Alex and took out her letters to reread. I won't be polite, she thought. I am tired of talk.

"Hey, Chang!" Jake called out. "Look, everyone."

They all turned to look at Chang, who stood in the middle of the room.

"What—what is wrong? Why yell and stare like barbarians?" he snapped.

"Your hat." Jake smiled.

"What wrong with hat?" Chang patted it carefully.

"It's your spring hat!"

Sarah looked. It was slightly less padded than his usual one, and a lighter color. She put down Goody's letter and said, "Do you always change hats when it gets warmer?"

" 'Course. Didn't lady notice wash water this morning?" He stared at her.

And Sarah smiled for the first time that day. "I guess I forgot. It wasn't frozen."

"The water's not frozen—hurrah, hurrah—soon we'll be going—hurrah, hurrah." Jake swung his fork.

"Going where?" Sarah asked.

"On the spring roundup. Got to brand the calves—best time of the year, Mrs. Proud." Jake munched on his pancakes. "We saddle up the horses," he said in a singsong voice, "and we set off to the foothills and up the gullies, and we ride and ride and drive the beeves onto the plain— And the food? God! The food makes your eyeballs pop out."

"That's enough," Alex said sharply.

"Boss?"

"That's enough. I don't want Sarah thinking about that roundup—"

"But don't the ranchers' wives help?" Sarah sat higher in her seat. I can ride a horse, then. I won't feel so small, then. Maybe I'll meet Calamity Jane, or even a neighbor. I might make a friend.

"Some do," he said shortly. "Ada never did, and I don't see why you should. It's bad company, Sarah. All cowboys, swearing and spitting, not for a lady's ears."

Sarah glared at him. "But I could cook, or—"

"No buts. I won't have it. It's too dangerous, too sweaty, too . . ."

Too much fun, Sarah wanted to spit. It's all right for me to share your bed—and your darn buttons. It's all right for me to cook with that man with the pigtail. It's all right to have frozen fingers and skate indoors, but when it comes to fun?

She snapped open Goody's letter and reread it.

"Watch out, boss," Fred said, quite soft. "Watch out."

After the dishes were washed, dried, and stacked on their shelf, Sarah threw off her apron and paced about the main room. Alex came up to her, holding her coat.

"Put this on."

"Why?"

"Do you have to be so ornery? Just put it on." But he smiled as he said it. He was dressed in riding clothes—melton coat and a wide, felt hat.

"Come on." He held the door open and tucked an apple in her pocket. Blitzen bounded past them and raced across the yard.

A sweet breeze blew. The snow was starting to melt, even since last night. Brown strips of land broke through the white. A few pools of water reflected the blue sky.

The buggy was already hitched and waiting. Alex helped her in, climbed up, and took the reins. He clucked to the horse and they rode down the track she'd come up three weeks before. Only three weeks, Sarah thought. And I have married, bedded, argued, cooked, skated, and frozen. She examined her hands.

103

"Sarah!" Alex nudged her. "Stop brooding and look up."

"I am *not* brooding."

"You are so. Now, look at that pasture there." He stopped the buggy and stood up. "That's mine." He spread his arm. "And the land goes all the way down to the foothills there"— he swung his arm back in a complete arc—"all the way to there." He chirruped to the horses and drove them onto a side track that cut across his land. The prairie rose before them in a gentle swell, like the back of a lion she'd seen in a picture— pale gold and wild.

"Why is there no snow here?" She pointed.

"The wind sweeps clean."

They rode on for a while in silence. Overhead, a hawk wheeled and cried. Something darted from a stand of pines and pounced on the grass.

"Fox," Alex said. "Prairie dog."

Sarah glared at him—talking like a telegraph message. "And, God willing, talk," indeed!

He pulled the horses to a stop and pointed. "There. What do you see?"

"Grass. Sky. Wind. Godawful loneliness."

Alex guffawed, surprised. "And what else, Miss Vinegar Mouth?"

Sarah stood in the buggy. Something dark wheeled against the lift of the hill and came toward them. It was one large horse—no, two—a bunch of horses racing across the grass.

Alex got down and held an apple out over the fence. "Here, boy, here."

A huge bay stallion thundered to a stop, earth clods flying to the side. Gently, he nibbled at the apple and took it in his mouth. Beside him, a smaller roan stuck her head over the fence and wiggled her lips.

"Give her the apple, Sary."

"Sarah." She held out the apple and the mare nuzzled her hand. Sarah laughed at the stiff hairs prickling her palm. The mare chomped up the apple, stepped closer, and put her head on Alex's shoulder.

"Ooh. How did you get her to do that? Will she put her head on my shoulder?" Sarah inched closer and the mare snorted and backed away.

"I trained her last fall." Alex smiled at her. "And when I knew you were coming, I fed her treats every day. Knew you'd need a horse of your own."

Sarah's eyes blurred and the line of the fence wavered. Just as she got up a head of steam to dislike him, he went and did something like this. Drat the man. You couldn't love *or* hate him, but something awful and bumpy in between.

"Don't you like her, Sary?" He took off his hat and scratched his ear.

" 'Course I like her." She sniffed and rubbed her nose quickly. "This is the best present I ever had. Ever." Since the china doll with the blue eyes Ma had given her on her tenth birthday.

"What will you call the mare?" He jammed his hat back on and whistled tunelessly.

Sarah thought for a minute. The horse pranced nearby, making small starts and leaps. "May" for the month? "Salvation" because she'd lasted three whole weeks here? "Joy" because spring was coming?

"I don't know. I'll know when I ride her."

Alex reached over, unhooked the gate, and slipped

105

through. Holding another apple, he coaxed the mare nearer and slipped a halter over her head. Rope in hand, he led the horse through the gate and tied her to the back of the buggy.

"Have to get you a sidesaddle," Alex said, as he helped Sarah onto the seat.

"Whatever for?"

"Well, Ada didn't like riding, so I never got her a saddle."

"Ada! I *like* horses and am a good rider. I'll use a regular saddle, none of those break-your-bottom sidesaddles for me."

"Sary!"

"Hush! Sarah. Now, let me drive for a change. Please," she added.

He handed her the reins and took a tight grip on the buggy's side. She flapped the reins against the horse's back and it broke into a trot. She took a quick look back—the mare followed easily on the lead with the dog beside. The wheels spun round and little drops of mud whirled into the air. She sniffed in the smell of wet earth and opened her mouth to the cool air. She felt the horse's live mouth through the reins, Alex beside her, and something sharp and sweet, like joy.

CHAPTER THIRTEEN

Sarah woke, scrunched to her side of the bed. She still wasn't used to sharing a bed, even after four weeks. She stared into the dark. An owl hooted. It must be early morning—she hadn't been asleep long. *This* was being married? Lying next to someone you didn't know who snored? He *was* kind, it was true. Sarah ticked off on one hand the good things about her marriage. A ranch. Not being a spinster. A dog. A horse. Montana and mountains. On the other hand, she ticked off all the bad things: this—this night business. She shook her finger. She kept seeing Ma in her coffin, furled like an umbrella in her black silk dress. Alex was at the end of his life, she at the beginning, and it wasn't right. She held up the next finger. Chang. Impertinent, yes, but she wasn't sure he was on the bad hand. He still stared at her and seemed to judge her. But ever since that day the water froze in the kitchen, he'd been nicer. The next finger. Godawful loneliness. No women friends. Even the ladies' sewing circle would be fine right now—even some talk about ague and dust would sound good. Surprised, Sarah held up her hands. The good side outbalanced the bad side. But no. This night thing was equal to two fingers, maybe even three.

Alex's snores grated on her ears. She could feel the heat rising from his body. His leg sprawled across on her side.

"Damn," she whispered, and got out of bed. Grabbing her clothes from the wall pegs, Sarah tiptoed into the main room. In front of the dying fire, she pulled on flannel underwear, the divided riding skirt she'd just bought, and layers of sweaters and a riding jacket. Blitzen pranced on his front feet, begging to come with her.

"All right, boy." She pushed open the front door and stood outside, breathing the cool early-morning air. Sweet, with no demands in it—just there for the taking. It calmed her, and she strode toward the barn with Blitzen following. Inside, the mare stomped a greeting and whickered. Sarah gave her a carrot to nibble and saddled her. She laid her head on the mare's neck and breathed in. A fresh, warm smell. An accepting smell, like a mother's lap.

Sarah led the horse out into the yard by the mounting block, stepped on it, and swung her leg over the mare's back. Then through the gate, close it, and off across the prairie. A cool scent of wetness and earth and new grass. Maine never smelled like this. Overhead, the Big Dipper glittered and shone. There were more stars here, she was sure, and they were brighter. She kept the mare to a jog, and thought, I shall call you Sophie, because you are comfortable as a sofa. Sarah felt they could go on and on without stopping, without tiring.

Whoo, hoo-whoo came from the trees ahead. A dark shape swept above, and a rabbit screamed. There was another sound, a soft whistle from the same band of trees. Sarah pulled the mare sharply to the right and kicked her hard. "Blitzen! Come!" That was a cat sound. Jake had told her about the sounds to watch out for, to be afraid of. "A woman screaming, is one," he said, "and a soft whistle is another—that's the mountain lion. Bears hoot, too, as they go along the foothills. Don't get in their way."

The mare flew over the prairie, the dog beside her, and Sarah opened her mouth wide. It felt good to let the air rush in, instead of keeping her lips tight together.

The ground changed, sloping up underneath. She slowed Sophie to a jog and peered ahead. The stars began to dim one by one, and a faint light lay on the horizon. Pines were dark shapes in front, and a breeze rustled up. Sarah stopped the horse. A tiny pinprick of red showed through the trees. Carefully, she rode nearer. Could be a mountain man. Jake had told her about them: loners—some drank—who crisscrossed the mountains looking for something and never finding it.

It *was* a fire. Sarah dismounted and tied Sophie's reins to a sturdy bush. Blitzen flopped down with a sigh. "Stay, boy," she whispered, and pushed through the trees.

There was a small fire. Near it sprawled two figures. They looked rough and unkempt, in tattered buckskins and moldy green hats. They snored and twitched like old dogs.

Sarah walked closer. Her foot cracked a stick, but the two figures did not stir. Dead to the world, she thought. There was an empty whiskey bottle by one of the bodies. Horses snuffled in the darkness and stomped their hooves.

"Dear me," Sarah said aloud. "Drunken old things."

Without warning, one of the figures sat up and spat.

"Not drunk, just tired," it croaked, and began to sing. " 'Had me a little girl, her name was Sal, prettiest thing in the whole dang val.' " He belched and held out a half-full bottle. "Want some, sweetheart? Can't tell if you *are* a sweetheart, though," he mumbled.

She shivered and stepped back. "No, thank you. Is that person—all right?" She pointed to the dead-looking figure.

"Her?" The man laughed raucously. "She *always* lands on her feet. She's tough as an old snake. Why, 'She's an old bull-whacker, an old rider,' " he began to sing.

Sarah hesitated. She should go. Goody always said, you can't tell what a drunken man might do. She'd better get out. Now.

The man stopped singing and peered at her. He had long golden hair, a scar down one cheek, and an assortment of ragged furs spread over his body.

"Ever see a mountain man before, gal?"

Sarah shook her head.

"Wal, there's not many of us left, now. Too settled up here for our taste. Seems everywhere you go you hear an ax, or a train. Anyhow"—he paused and drank from the bottle— "you're seeing one now. Mountain Jim. No one tells *me* what to do, no sir. I got no boss. Not much money, either," he snorted, "but enough for the good things in life." He drank and propped his hat over his eyes.

Sarah thought he'd nodded off, but suddenly, his voice rang out. "You know what the good things in life are, gal?"

Sarah took a deep breath. "Of course, I . . . ."

He broke in, "Wine, women, and song. Also horses. Mountains, too. And a dog, if you got one. Know who that is?" He pointed to the still figure.

Sarah stepped closer. The face was ravaged. Once beautiful, with dark hair and sharp cheekbones, it looked like the world had rolled over it. Then, something in the face made her come closer. That dark hair? Those large eye sockets?

"No—it can't be. . . ."

"Surely is. Calamity Jane!" He hooted and slapped his thigh. "Best woman God ever made. Give you the shirt off her back and never ask for it again, no sir." He patted the woman's hand. "Drinks a bit, 'course, but she's no housewife. No sitting indoors waiting for her man to come home. No sweeping floors, no sir."

Sarah stared. It—she, was dressed in man's clothes. Not at all glamorous. Not at all like the picture on the front of *Beadle's Pocket Library*. "Heroine of Whoop-Up," indeed. Her mouth was open and she snored.

"How did she—what happened to her?" Sarah crouched by the woman.

Mountain Jim drank, wiped his mouth on his hat, and set it back on his head. "World don't allow for different kinds of women, gal. You're either a loose one, like her—or a respectable one, like you. It puts you in boxes and don't allow nothing in between."

Sarah stood quickly. He didn't know what he was talking about—drunken old man!

The man began to laugh. "Go back to your house, young thing. She's too rich for your blood, I can tell. Go on, git!"

Sarah turned and ran through the bushes, grabbed Sophie's reins, and was off, with Blitzen just behind. The wind blew in her face and the horizon was a pale red.

That was being free? Free to get drunk and get rained on? Free to wear moldy old hats and smell? Sarah patted the mare's neck for comfort. But still, no one told Calamity Jane what to do. She dressed as she pleased, came and went as she pleased. Was that better than living with a man old enough to be your grandfather?

Sarah slowed Sophie to a walk to keep from getting home too fast.

When she and Blitzen crept into the house, she saw the rocker moving, rocking by the fire. Sarah put her hand to her chest. Ada? Come back to haunt her for being ungrateful?

Then a voice came out of the dark. "Where were you? I was worried." It was Alex.

Sarah sighed and walked to the fire. "I took Sophie for a ride. I couldn't sleep."

"Oh, Sarah, at night? Alone? Did you hear any bears?"

"No."

"Panthers?"

"Mmm—"

"Sary, you've got to be more careful. This isn't Maine, you can't just roam around out there, it isn't safe. . . ."

"I was perfectly safe. I had Blitzen, I was on my horse. . . ."

"I wonder if I should have given you a horse. You should be wiser about how you use her." He rose and stood beside her.

"It's not wise for me to be cooped up all day, Alex."

"How can you be cooped up? A ranch, barns, acres and acres of prairie—"

"But you don't want me to *roam* about it, Alex. Calamity Jane roams about, and she's come to no harm." There, almost out, but she'd not tell about their meeting.

"Calamity Jane!" He sat down and pushed the rocker back and forth. "She's a drunk, Sarah, not fit to associate with ladies."

"Ladies—that's what I came out here to escape. Sitting

and sewing, sitting and rocking, talking about hymn sings and knitting dusters for Africans."

He rocked faster. "Ada didn't mind sewing and being in the house."

"Ada!" She rapped her heels on the hearthstones. "Ada was not well. I am. I thought you wanted a companion, Alex, not a drudge. I distinctly did *not* read 'drudge' in the advertisement." She stalked off to the kitchen, began clattering pans, and did not hear Alex say, "Sary?" and then leave for his chores in the barn.

CHAPTER FOURTEEN

"No."

"But, Alex, other women go on the spring roundup. Jake told me."

"Jake! I don't care about other women, Sarah. What if you're in a delicate—"

"I am *not* pregnant," Sarah said. "I could cook, Alex."

"Chang will cook."

"I could help keep the cattle together. . . ."

"No. It's too dangerous. You'll stay here with Blitzen. I've shown you how to use the Winchester, if you need it. Though, God knows, you're safer here than just about anywhere."

Sarah got out of bed, lit the lamp, and dressed in its flickering light. She looked quickly at Alex, dressing on the other side of the room. His back was straight and stubborn. She could hurl arrows at it and it wouldn't make any difference. Maybe that was why Calamity Jane had ended up a drunken woman wearing moldy hats. Maybe she'd been married to someone like Alex. Sarah threw on a sweater and left the room.

She heard pots clattering in the kitchen, as Chang prepared supplies for the spring roundup. Sarah kicked a log in the living room fire and it showered sparks onto the hearth. She threw a piece of oak onto the embers and blew. Alex didn't know it yet, but she was going. She wouldn't stay here like some drudge, taking orders from him. What had Mountain Jim said two weeks ago? "I got no boss. No one tells *me* what to do." She'd be like that, only not drunk. It was time to start putting her foot down, time to be independent.

She went into the kitchen and put on the coffeepot.

"Hello, lady." Chang stuck a chunk of salt pork onto brown paper and wrapped it carefully. Sarah picked up the containers of salt, sugar, and coffee and packed them in canvas sacks.

Chang frowned. "Hate roundups. Food burns. Bugs bite. Panthers make noises."

"I wish I were going," Sarah said shortly.

Chang adjusted his hat. "Why lady want to go? Nice here—calm and quiet. A rest from hairy men who eat too much."

Sarah laughed. "Is that how you see them?"

Chang nodded. "So big—so smelly—eat like horses, sound like horses."

Suddenly, Sarah saw things through Chang's eyes—as if someone had put a stereoscope to her eyes and both pictures became one. We must be like moon men to him.

"Are you happy here, Chang?" She heard the echo of Alex's question a month ago.

"Happy? What is happy?" Chang put wood on the fire. "In China, is not word we use. Enough to eat?" *Slam* went the wood. "Children by door?" *Bam* went the stove lids. "Pig in backyard?"

Maybe I want too much. Sarah sipped her coffee. Maybe I should be more like Chang—food, animals, and family. "Do you like it better here than in China?"

"Yes. Quiet here, not too many people. Home was full

of people, like thousand bugs on log. Never enough to eat. Hot in summer, freezing in winter. Here is open—is free."

"What do you miss from home?"

He smoothed down his plait and was silent for a moment. "Pickled vegetables—and lotus flowers."

The door banged open, and William, Fred, and Jake tumbled into the house.

"Chang? Where's breakfast? We're hungry as wolves!" For the next half-hour, the house was filled with the clatter of men's boots and excited talk of the roundup, as Sarah and Chang flew back and forth, putting out food.

And suddenly, they were gone. Alex gave her a quick peck on her cheek: "Be good, my dear, we'll miss you. Make sure you keep Blitzen close, he'll take care of you." Jake winked, and they were gone.

Sarah stood in the doorway and waved. Chang sat on the buckboard, shoulders slumped, holding grimly to the reins of the bays. Fred and Jake mounted their horses and rode through the gate with high yells.

"Whee-yup. Hi-yi-yi!"

Sarah wanted to be there, on Sophie, shouting with the rest. See you later, she almost yelled. Soon she'd be on her way. No more staying at home, like a piece of china on a shelf. *She* was going on the roundup and would show how useful she could be.

"Whee-yup!" Alex yelled.

And from the doorway, Sarah waved and shouted, "Hi-yi-yi-yi!"

She gave them a two-day start on the roundup. Give Alex

a chance to relax, thinking I'm safe at home. *Then* I'll join them.

Early the third morning, she dressed in the divided riding skirt, a thick warm shirt and sweater, and a loose duster jacket. She tied on a hat to protect her from the sun and looked in the cracked mirror over the dresser. Her face was shaded by the hat, as it had been in the picture she'd sent Alex in the spring. She pressed her cheeks with her fingers. Was she the same person? The person who put gunpowder into the school stove? The person who put molasses on the minister's saddle? Could she possibly be the same person who stole the men's clothes and made Charlie Blackmun crawl home naked? She'd thought she was brave—and daring. Now she thought it was something else. Something like "foolishness," as Goody would call it. In the mirror she saw Pa waving one black-clothed arm as she left for Montana. She saw Goody sitting on her bed, candle flickering, as she tried to explain married life. All of those scenes were disconnected, like beads fallen off a string. There didn't seem to be anything connecting her past life to this one. "Except me," Sarah said. "Except me."

"Come, Blitzen." She patted her hat and strode into the kitchen. Into a canvas saddlebag she put dried apples, salt pork, oatmeal, and cold corn cakes. Sarah caught Sophie from the corral with a pail of grain and saddled her quickly. She tied a roll of wool blankets behind the saddle and hooked the canteen and canvas bag over the pommel. Mounting, she set off through the gate and closed it, Blitzen racing ahead. Then off she went, the grass rushing by below. She was a boat sailing over a green sea. A balloon floating across a green sky. No one could get at her or stop her. Up to the pines, across a small, swift brook, up a low hill she rode.

117

"First four foothills," the men had said one night at supper. "It's half a day's ride up the first two, then through one ravine, up to the higher foothills, and that's where we start getting the cattle to bring down to the plain."

She rode all afternoon, over the prairie that seemed the same and yet always changing. Up the gradual slope of one hill, through the green grasses speckled with yellow, orange, and blue flowers, down the other side. Through valleys with clear streams, past small stands of pine where the shadows smelled fresh and cool, up another slope to the top. Hawks wheeled lazily overhead. Nowhere, Sarah thought, nowhere else could I find country like this—open and free, with just grass and trees and air. Under a tall pine she stopped for lunch and to let the mare graze. She fed Blitzen some cold corn cakes and a hunk of salt pork. Then on again, as the sun circled lower in the sky. She kicked Sophie to a canter and they sped down the fourth foothill, through a rocky valley where mule deer slept in the shade and did not race away, up another slope.

She heard them before she saw them. The noisy bawling of the cattle, the muffled sound of hooves on grass. Above the bawling, she heard a few human shouts: "Whee-up! Git, there, git!" and someone swearing long and colorfully.

She topped the last rise, the dog trailing wearily behind, and saw Jake riding pell-mell down a hill, driving five cattle before him. "Whee-up! Git!" The cattle they had already collected milled about a mountain pasture. She could see brown backs, russet backs, horns swinging from side to side. William and Fred, on their horses, watched over the herd of cows and kept them from straying.

Sarah trotted alongside the jostling herd until she reached Fred.

"'Lo."

"Ma'am!" He touched his hat. "Does Mr. Proud know you're here?"

"Not yet." She smiled.

"Am I glad to see you! I was just thinking of your buttermilk biscuits and what we'd have tonight—stringy beef. But Mr. Proud'll be mad. You'd better stay back here with me. He's over there"—he pointed to a ravine below—"getting a few wild ones."

The sun edged down to the horizon in a blaze of red and orange. Ahead of them rose the sharp points of the Rockies, white on top, shading to blue. Sarah felt calm and rested, and thought, There's nothing to this cattle business. Just keep your seat on your horse and all's well. Suddenly, the cattle nearby jostled and bawled, and one black cow swung her horns viciously at Sarah.

"Watch out!" The dog darted to one side as Fred rode his horse between the cow and Sarah. "You'd better stay farther back, ma'am. If anything happened to you, boss'd . . ." He drew his finger across his throat.

Sarah patted her handkerchief against her forehead. So quick. Those horns could gore a horse, the hooves trample a man, or a woman. She shivered and thought of Calamity Jane. *She* wouldn't be afraid—she'd be out here on a horse, yelling and whooping right with the men.

Just below, she saw Alex riding his big gray stallion, charging up the hill with three calves and a roan cow in front. He hadn't seen her yet. She waved to William and he waved back, from his position on the edge of the meadow. Chang had started a fire, and she could see him moving between buckboard and fire. A plume of thin blue smoke rose upward.

Jake herded his cows in with the rest and rode up to her. "Hello, there—a welcome sight!" He dismounted and helped her down, grinning. "Good for you," he said, and filled a pail of water for Sophie. Sarah let the dog drink first. William unpacked her horse and made inarticulate welcoming sounds.

Alex pushed the calves into the herd with one last "whee-up!" and rode over to them. "What're you doing here? You should be at home. Is anything wrong?" Blitzen leaped on Alex, paws flailing.

"There's nothing wrong, Alex. I just wanted to be here with you, that's all."

"Well." He snapped his mouth shut and frowned. "You can't go back tonight. Sarah, this isn't time for a child's prank. I'll have to spare one of the men to take you back tomorrow—"

"I'm not going back, Alex. I'm staying here with you. I'll cook and—and help watch." She didn't feel so certain, saying it, and repeated it firmly. "Help watch."

Alex paused and noticed the men standing around, listening to their argument. Jake made a pretense of rubbing down Sophie.

"We'll talk about it later." Alex strode away to tend to his gray stallion.

Sarah went over to Chang. He was mixing corn cakes in a tin pail.

"Let me help."

He grunted and nodded his head at a package. Sarah sawed off hunks of salt pork and set them to fry in an iron pan. She filled the coffeepot from the pail William brought her and set it on the edge of the fire. She felt like a dog turning around in the grass to make a place. The shadows reached across the meadow, and the sky was a pale, icy green. Sarah sniffed the air and grinned at Chang. He smiled back. This was better than cleaning house. This was better than being in the kitchen at home. It was worth braving Alex's anger to be outside with the night coming in and the wind blowing sweet. Resolutely, she pushed aside the image of the cow with its horns swinging viciously.

After they had eaten and cleaned up, the men sat by the fire and stretched out their legs. William handed round a pouch of tobacco, and they rolled their own cigarettes.

"Ever hear of the time that panther got our best breeder, ma'am?" Fred asked. He did not hand her the tobacco.

"No." She spread her skirts and toasted her feet. Alex took her hand and pulled her up.

"Come on. You're coming with me." He led her beyond the campfire, out of earshot.

"I've made excuses for you because you are young." He put his hand on her shoulder. "I've said, give her time, this is so far away, so new. But this is enough, Sarah."

"You're right, it is enough." Sarah stuck out her chin. "I'm tired of being in the house all the time, Alex. There's no reason why I can't help out here. Calamity Jane used to drive cows—why, she even fought in the Indian Wars."

"*She* says. Calamity Jane." He spat. "Why, she's just a drunk, Sarah. If she ever fell off a horse, she wouldn't even feel it. Can't you see that it's dangerous out here? These cows are wild—they've been up in the ravines and gullies all winter, getting wild and ornery. There's no telling—"

"There's no telling what I might do, Alex, if I don't get out more."

Alex began to tear off pine branches for his bed. He threw some down near Sarah. "I don't understand you. Ada didn't want to be here on the roundup. She wanted to be inside—"

"Alex!" She tried to keep her voice calm and took a deep breath. Be careful what you say about his dead wife. "Ada was an invalid—I guess. I am not. You don't know what it's like to get up in the morning and tussle with that dratted stove and cook the same meals over and over."

"Then let Chang cook. That's what he's here for." He unrolled his blankets on the pine bed.

Sarah flapped her arms. "You just don't understand, do you? It's the sameness, Alex. Every day alike as beads on a string. I'll go crazy. I'll tear my clothes off and run naked through town!"

"Sarah!" He looked at her and then started to laugh. "You —you think I deceived *you* with that picture? What about me?"

Sarah flung her blankets down on the bed.

"Didn't I advertise for a woman of 'docile temper'?"

Sarah did not answer, rolled up in the blankets, and lay down. She turned her back to him.

He sighed. "Maybe I was too old to marry again. Maybe it was a mistake. If you really want to stay, you can. But I think it's dangerous and foolish, and if you get hurt . . ."

"I won't." Sarah folded her jacket for a pillow. Behind her, Alex sighed and lay down on his bed. Overhead, the stars glittered and shone. A wind rustled up like silk. She could hear Alex turning uncomfortably. From time to time he sighed. Suddenly she thought, Victory is not sweet; it's like eating the pickle after maple sugar.

122

CHAPTER FIFTEEN

She heard the cattle stomping and whuffing. Sounds of breath escaping, and small grunts from cows and their calves. Overhead, the stars ran in a white stream from one mountain to another.

Sarah stood in the dark, swinging her arms. Alex was gone, and she was here—on her own—away from the house, away from kitchens and stoves and scrubbing. She pushed through the wet meadow, grass slapping her skirt. The fire from last night still glowed. She threw on another juniper log and watched the sparks sail through the air. Like her. Free. Humming, she picked up a pail and went along the meadow's edge to the stream, Blitzen at her heels. The wind blew her hair back. It was crisp and cool as the stream water. "Snow, Blitzen, we will have coffee made from melted snow." She grinned. There was nothing tired, nothing old about this land. Not all used up, like Maine, with the sound of axes and trains and too many voices chattering. For the moment, Sarah forgot how she'd wished for the sound of another girl's voice.

She heard Jake and Alex calling to the cattle, keeping them together with their horses. There was a faint edge of light along the pasture, and the dark shapes of cattle milled against it. Sarah remembered how Jake had smiled, talking of the spring roundup. He knew something she had not: that being outdoors with a dog at your knee and the wind blowing was as sweet as love.

She filled the coffeepot and set it on the edge of the fire. Red now showed along the horizon, and a small bird *pinged* nearby. Cattle tore off grass with slow, munching sounds. Blitzen stood, nose into the wind, listening.

Suddenly, Jake was beside her. "You startled me!" Sarah steadied the coffeepot on its rock.

"I aim to startle, ma'am." She could just see his smile in the light.

"You're awake early," he said, and squatted beside her.

"It's too beautiful to sleep."

"Mmm." Jake stood, scooped some water from the pail, rubbed his face vigorously, then wiped it on his sleeve. "Beautiful's too soft a word, I'd say."

"Yes, it is." She watched the flames lick up the sides of the pot and heard some cattle rumble across the pasture, chasing each other. Sarah stood and got supplies and a frying pan from the canvas sack. By the fire, she sliced up salt pork and set it to fry.

"Words don't do it," Jake said. "They never did. A word just gets lost out here, like an ant in an elephant's ear."

Sarah laughed. Soon, Fred and William joined them, their hair sticking out from sleep. She handed them cold corn cakes from last night and watched them mount their horses to ride along the edge of the herd. For a moment, she thought of them as brothers—Fred, Jake, and William a family, and she was their sister. Chang arrived, a neat, washed figure in contrast to the shaggy hands. He crouched by the fire and reheated corn cakes from last night.

Alex dismounted and came over, rubbing his hands. "Well, this isn't so bad—salt pork, coffee, fried corn cakes."

Sarah glanced at him. Good. He wasn't going to sulk or

hold a grudge. He'd come over to her way of thinking, at least a little bit, and now saw how useful she'd be. She tossed some salt pork to the dog before serving the others.

They ate quickly, talking of the day's chores. "Half a day's ride," Alex said, "to get the rest of the calves down from the hills. We'll head back now."

"Same as yesterday?" Jake asked.

"The same," Alex said. "Fred and William are already mounted. Sarah, you'll drive the herd with them, while Jake and I search out the rest. Chang, you follow us in the buckboard and catch up with us."

He nodded and went to wash dishes in the meadow stream.

Alex saddled her horse and held out his hands for Sarah. "Remember, now," he said tightly, "no getting in the middle of the herd. I don't want you scaring any of the cows or separating them. Stick by Fred and do what he does—otherwise, I'll take you back home myself."

"Of course, Alex, I know that!" She stepped on his hands and he lifted her on top of Sophie.

"Come on, ma'am." Fred rode up to her. "You and me go around back and get them started."

She whistled to Blitzen, and they followed Fred down the side of the meadow, keeping at the edge of the herd. "Don't get into the herd," Fred cautioned. "We don't want them going in different directions."

The cattle smell was strong and pungent, a leathery, warm smell that pricked her nose. The cattle hardly looked at Sarah and Fred as they reached the bottom of the meadow and began to swing their arms and shout.

"Whee-up! Gee-up! Come on, there!"

Sarah shouted with him. "Whee-up! Gee-up! Come on, there!" Blitzen rushed at their heels, barking. The cattle began to move, slowly at first, the back ones pushing against the ones in front. Horns tossed, a calf bawled, and suddenly the herd was moving—a brown mass of backs and horns and thick, wet noses.

"Whee-up! Gee-up! Come on, there!" Sarah yelled. It was a song, a rhythm, she, Sophie, and the dog moved to. They trotted behind the cows, urging them on. Fred looked over and grinned at her, and William waved from across the herd. No one could talk—it was too noisy now, with the bawling and mooing and thundering hooves. Down through the meadow they surged, past stands of tall pines, down a rocky ravine. The herd rattled down the sharp incline, and they followed. Sophie bunched her legs and half-slid down the hill. Sarah sat back in the saddle and let the reins loosen. Not far away, Fred did the same. He shouted, "All right?" to her. Sarah saw his lips move, and she smiled and nodded.

They flowed down the slope, reached a narrow bottom where a stream glittered, and the herd splashed through and up the other side. It was partly wooded and grassy. All Sarah could see was cattle—brown backs, russet backs, spotted backs flowing downhill. She caught a glimpse of Jake on one side, herding two calves toward the main body of the herd, but saw no one else. Up the hill they scrambled, ducking under tree limbs, and out into the sun of another meadow. The cattle wanted to graze, but they urged them on.

"Whee-up! Gee-up! Come on, there!" Sarah's voice was hoarse. Her hair was straggling out from her hat, and her eyes stung from the dust kicked up by the cows. But she swayed in the saddle and grinned, all the way to the top of the hill.

Blitzen kept close by Sophie's heels, barking importantly. A cool wind blew, and ahead Sarah saw the shoulders of two more foothills they must cross—light green where grassy, dark green where trees grew. She plunged after the herd as they scrambled down the other side of the hill. She saw Fred trying to work his way closer to her, shouting and whipping his horse. He got close enough to yell, "Be careful! Ravine to your left!"

The meadow ran up to a rocky edge below, and she could see a dark space between that edge and the lift of the hill beyond. A hawk soared above, then disappeared into the ravine. She caught her breath.

She nudged Sophie to a trot and started over the hilltop. Fred and William were farther away now, and she could just see Alex to her left. He was riding to the side of a rangy cow, whose calf followed close beside. He looked happy—head up, swinging a coil of rope, and leaning forward in his saddle.

She watched him guide the cow carefully and skillfully, always keeping the calf close by. Then, suddenly the calf separated from the cow. It scooted off to one side, heading for the ravine. Its mother broke away after it, head swinging. Alex turned his horse and followed—too fast, Sarah thought. He's doing his daredevil act, she thought, chasing his cows, pretending he's twenty years younger.

As she clutched the saddle pommel for balance, she saw Alex riding along the ravine's edge. The calf was ahead, the roan just behind. Alex's arm swung out with a coil of rope, and the calf skidded to a stop. The cow piled up beside it, and suddenly, the horse lost its balance. Its back feet slipped on the scree and scrabbled at the ravine edge. Alex let go of the rope, leaned forward to help the horse, but in one sudden motion, the hindquarters slid over the edge, and horse and rider disappeared.

"Alex!" Sarah turned her mare hard to the left. Along the edge of the herd she trotted, not daring to canter, until she came nearer the ravine. Blitzen raced ahead, barking. Cautiously, she let Sophie pick her way closer until she could look over the edge. Maybe he'd just fallen a little way, or managed to leap off and catch a root or branch. Sarah looked over the edge. The earth fell away in a jagged gash. No trees, nothing to break a fall. Far below, where the stream glittered, was a black shape like a tangled star.

Fred rode up to her side. "Now, missus, now, missus," he repeated in a hoarse voice. "Come back from that edge." He reached out, grabbed Sophie's reins, and led them away from the ravine.

The herd went on without them, stumbling, sliding, bawling their way down the hill, up the other side. Fred said, "Now, you wait here. Don't do a thing. I'm going down into the ravine to see—to see—"

"He can't be alive, Fred," Sarah said flatly. "It's too far a fall. You could tell."

"All the same, I'm going down, just to see." He left, and Sarah dismounted, tying Sophie to a tree. She was glad to rest there, away from the noise of the cattle. She felt dizzy and sat suddenly on the grass. The dog nosed her arm and whined. She watched the animals reach the top of the next foothill, a brown wave against green. Then they stopped. Small figures on horses rode around the edges, like insects on a hide. Must be Jake and William, keeping the herd together. One insect zigzagged down the hill toward the bottom of the ravine. Time passed. A hawk flew overhead. Light blazed through his pin-

128

ions, and she could hear the wind rushing past his wings. She heard the sound of a rifle and jerked back. The horse. Then the insect reappeared and started up the hill toward her. It grew larger, like something from a fever nightmare. Fred. And his horse strained under an extra weight.

"Nothing we could do," Fred was saying. He rode closer, panting and steaming. "Nothing we could do.

"It was a clean fall," he said. "No suffering, ma'am."

She looked quickly at the shape behind him, with the red bandanna around his neck. Alex looked smaller, and somehow younger. Below them, the others rode along the edges of the herd, bunching it together. They were waiting.

Then she heard the clatter of the buckboard and looked back. Chang had caught up with them and stood in the wagon as he came up.

"What happen?" He looked from Sarah to Fred.

"He . . ." Fred began.

"Alex fell. . . ." Sarah said.

"I see that!" Chang snapped, and leaped off the seat. He went up to Fred's horse, lifted Alex across his back, and carried him to the buckboard. He laid him carefully in the bottom, folding a jacket under Alex's head. Chang's lips were tightly pressed together, and two tears rolled down his cheeks.

He climbed onto the seat and turned to Sarah. "Lady all right?"

"All right?" She let out one great sob. All right to lose a man much nicer than Pa and anyone else in Dewborne? All right to be all alone in the middle of Montana Territory with a ranch and hands and a thousand cattle?

She put her hand to her chest, kicked Sophie, and said, "Let's go home."

129

CHAPTER SIXTEEN

Ever after, Sarah remembered that homecoming as a mixture of cries and silence. The cattle bawled their way onto the plain near the ranch and milled about in the end-of-day light. The silence was from her and Fred and William, Jake and Chang. There were no human sounds—just moos and bawling and the click of hooves on stone. All the way back, Sarah kept from looking at the buckboard with its extra burden. And when they stopped, the hands had all they could do to get the cattle into two big corrals. It was Chang and Sarah who carried Alex into the house, arms under his shoulders. It was Chang who put Alex down on the bunk and said to Sarah, "Go wash face. I make coffee. Go." He patted her shoulder. And Sarah, though she meant to stay up, fell into a stunned sleep as soon as she sat on her bed, dropping back fully dressed with her face still grimed from the ride.

The next morning, Sarah rose early and went into the main room. Chang looked weary but satisfied, as he smoothed Alex's hair with a wet cloth.

"There. He all ready."

Sarah touched Chang's hand briefly—gratefully. "Thank you, Chang." Thank God, Alex looked normal—a little bruised, but with no awful wounds.

Chang went on, "I told you, I take care of Mr. Proud. I not let busy ladies from town talk and clean my Mr. Proud.

No, sir. No, sir." Chang adjusted Alex's neckcloth and stood back. He seemed pleased with his work.

To Sarah, Alex looked asleep, yet not asleep—the features the same, the body arranged to look like a sleeper. But something was gone. She pressed closer. Something around the mouth, something around the eyes, as if what made a person alive rested there, just under the surface, and once you were dead, it flew away.

"Do you believe in souls, Chang?"

"Mmmph! Not sure about souls. Once believed in demons, until Mr. Proud taught me. We think ancestors live on. Burn incense to ancestors to keep them happy."

Maybe he was alive somewhere, riding a horse. Or riding his big gray stallion around the edge of the ranch, keeping an eye on things. It made her feel safe, yet creepy.

They sat down to a silent breakfast—William, Jake, and Fred. It was only broken when William said in his quiet voice, "Guess we'll have to cut out the calves today, ma'am."

"Have to brand them." Jake brightened. "Can't leave so many beeves just milling about, ma'am. They drop a lot of weight that way."

Sarah wiped her mouth. "Whatever you say. Do what you need to do. We'll let the neighbors know about Alex and—and . . ."

Chang stood next to her and said, "And have funeral here late today."

Sarah looked at her hands. "I'll get the food ready. We do need food, don't we, Chang?" She looked to him, and he nodded.

"Very important to have enough food at funeral—for honor of house."

The men pushed back their chairs and disappeared outside, while Chang hitched up the buggy and drove off to get the minister and tell the neighbors of Alex's death.

All morning Sarah baked, staying in the hot kitchen, staying away from the bed where Alex seemed to be napping. She felt tired, with a weariness that started in her chest bones, spreading out. Only the sight of her cakes and pies, added to those Chang had made the night before, comforted her.

Chang returned that afternoon, dusty and long-faced, with an empty coffin in the buggy. He just had time to wash and help Sarah get ready when they heard the clatter of hobnailed boots on the floor. The front door opened and shut, opened and shut. She'd have to go out and greet her neighbors—people she'd never met. She'd have to be a sorrowful widow, whatever *that* was.

"Do I look all right, Chang?" Nervously, she adjusted her dark blue dress and the lace cuffs. She didn't own a mourning dress.

Chang brushed a speck off her shoulder and said, "All right, lady. Go out and don't talk. Just sigh and serve whiskey. Everyone have good time, then, and say, 'Mrs. Proud did right by her husband.' "

Sarah went through the bedroom door into the living room, where they had set up long tables covered with pies and cakes.

"Hello, Mrs. Proud." A stout woman dabbed at her eyes. "I'm so sorry for your loss, so sorry. He was a good man, Mr. Proud."

"Yes." Sarah nodded and sighed. "Yes." It was hard to hear over the bawling of the cattle outside.

"I'm sorry we didn't meet sooner," the woman shouted.

"I'm Mrs. Wheeler and we have the ranch eight miles down the road. We were planning to come over and visit, but you know how it is—the snow keeps us in, then the roundup . . . some of our boys are out there helping yours cut out the calves. The boys'll be in later."

Sarah nodded again.

"Mrs. Proud—what a sad occasion!" another woman bellowed. Sarah recognized her as the hotelkeeper from Dillman two months ago. A familiar face! "Little did I know when I saw you that next time you'd be a widow. Deary me, deary me." The woman's sympathy flowed over her like molasses, and Sarah plucked at her top button. It was hot in here, close, with too many people. She'd gotten used to mountains and ravens for company. Now she was surrounded. She thought of Calamity Jane lying out in the open and envied her.

After everyone had had a chance to see Alex, Chang and Jake lifted the body into the wooden coffin and closed the lid. Sarah felt breathless and scared, as if the lid had come down over her own face. She followed them outdoors. People parted like waves to make room as the two men bore Alex to a spot about a hundred feet from the house, under a large pine. A small white stone marked Ada's grave. The hole Fred and Jake had dug early that morning gaped in the sunshine.

Jake strung ropes under the foot and head of the coffin, and the neighbors hurried to help lower Alex into the grave. Dirt slid down the sides of the hole. The minister took up a position in the shade and began to read from his Bible, shouting to be heard over the sound of the cattle.

The words flowed over Sarah. All she saw were faces—dark, leathery faces—flushed, red faces—tired faces—a child's curious look at the grave—a baby basking in the sun. What

133

did they know of Alex? What did *she* know? Next to nothing. She clenched her hands. Next to nothing. How he snored. What his feet sounded like on the floorboards in the morning. That sometimes he would rather give in than fight. That he liked his whiskey neat from a tumbler. That he combed his moustache with a curve-handled comb. That he liked Scott's novels. That he thought Sarah was, what? Too young? Too small and plain? Too sharp-tongued?

"Ashes to ashes, dust to dust" rose above the cattle sounds. Jake threw a clod of dirt into the grave, and the men began to shovel, putting their backs into it.

That he *liked* you, came suddenly to Sarah. He thought you were fun—"Miss Vinegar Mouth." She pressed a handkerchief to her mouth and was afraid she'd throw up or cry. She wasn't sure which was worse.

People looked at her curiously, mournfully. Many patted her shoulder as they went by. But it was Chang who led her into the house, and it was Jake who appeared at her elbow and handed her a small shot glass of whiskey. "Jake, I can't. I've never had whiskey straight."

"This is a good time to start," Jake said. "I've already had some myself—danged crowds," he muttered. "Now drink up, ma'am, you look too pale for my taste." He was still dusty from working with the cattle and had obviously just wiped a cloth across his face. Traces of dirt striped his eyes.

Sarah sniffed at the whiskey. It smelled sour and fieldy. She sipped cautiously, coughed, and looked around.

Everyone seemed to be drinking, even the ladies in their starched black dresses or best calico, holding their glasses daintily and sliding the whiskey into their mouths like it was evil but delicious. Sarah sipped again, and the whiskey burned its way down her throat.

"Ma'am." The minister took her elbow. "Such a sad loss. We loved Mr. Proud. He did a lot for Dillman—paid for the bell in the church, gave money to the fund for widows and orphans. He was a true Charistian gentleman."

Sarah peered at the black-clothed figure over the rim of her glass. Just like the one at Ma's funeral. If he said one word, *one word* about it being a blessing and Mr. Proud being in heaven, she'd throw the whiskey in his face.

He stepped back a pace, murmured, "Sad loss," and hurried away.

Sarah went to the window and looked out. In the corral, men were helping to brand High Ridge's calves. There was William on his horse, cutting out a stubby calf, roping it swiftly and jumping to the ground. Another man ran up and branded the calf's hide. She could see the smoke puff up. The animal bawled and then ran, stiff-legged, to its mother.

She saw William dismount, wipe his face, and head for the house with another man.

Sarah gulped the last of the whiskey as Jake appeared with another glass for her. "Is it all right—out there?"

He nodded. "Everyone's helping. We'll be done by sundown and then let the beeves loose."

Alex should be here, she thought, branding his own calves—his own work. She shook her head. "Who are all these people, Jake?"

"Ranchers—townspeople." He pointed them out. The fat man with a black waistcoat and gold chain stretched to breaking was the banker. His wife was thin and nervous, fiddling with her brooch. The tall man in a brown jacket by the door was their neighbor, Mr. Halley. He had the land adjoining theirs, with three thousand head of cattle. "Lost half his herd that bad winter four years back," Jake said. "Minister's wife," he whispered, nodding toward a sturdy woman in a blue-striped dress. "She runs that family—will of iron."

Sarah drank again and wondered at the ladies. None seemed like fainting violets. Most looked tough and windburned, and their faces flushed redder as the day wore on.

A man in a tight brown suit walked up to her as someone tuned a violin. "Mrs. Proud?" He stuck out his hand and gave hers a firm shake. "I'm Mr. Delon, the lawyer from town. Your husband left his will in my keeping."

The man rubbed his nose and smiled.

Sarah stared at him stupidly. She drank again and said, "And?"

"Well, I s'pose we should wait until we read the will in my office, but *who's* to read the will to?" He rocked back and forth on his heels. "It's all yours, ma'am. All two thousand acres—cattle, outbuildings, the works."

"It is?" Sarah patted her collar. The lace itched her throat. "Mine? High Ridge?"

"Yours. High Ridge. Now, don't you fret yourself about it." He rocked faster on his heels. "I'll help you find a buyer. What a generous man Mr. Proud was. You'll get a good price for the ranch and can go back East, ma'am, a rich and pr"— he stopped himself—"a rich and young widow."

Sarah felt dizzy and leaned against the wall. The lawyer wandered away, and someone lifted a violin and began to play. The minister led them in singing "Onward, Christian Soldiers." Then they sang "Amazing Grace" and "Heavenly Man-

136

sions." Sarah's head ached with the noise, and her mouth was too dry to sing. She swayed back and forth. Everything blurred in the most disconcerting way. The banker looked swollen like a black balloon—his wife like a sick green hanky. People's faces were huge and grotesque, their eyes black and beady. Sarah clutched her throat and swayed against the wall.

Suddenly, Chang was at her side. "Lady come into room and lie down. This too much for you." She heard Chang say, "Lady overcome by sadness," to someone and let herself be led into the bedroom.

Chang loosened her dress collar and gave her a glass of water. "Sit on bed, lady." She obeyed. The room seemed to be rotating. "Put head between knees." She hung her head, and the blood rushed down. It felt warm—and sad. She began to cry, snuffling between her knees.

"He was a good man, Chang—a good man. Old—but good." She sniffed.

"Yes, he was old—but good." Chang patted her arm. "That Jake!" he hissed. "You ever drink before, lady?"

"No," Sarah moaned, and rocked back and forth. "Never. Aunt Goody said only devils drink, and I was a worse enough devil already." She began to sob—for Goody and her kind hands, for the familiar kitchen at home.

"Such a mess, Chang. I've made a mess—ever since I got here." She rocked back and forth, and Chang sat down beside her. He touched her shoulder.

"Nonsense—lady talk nonsense! It not easy come West to old rancher man. Not easy. Chang think you do very well."

She sniffed. "You do?"

"Yes, very well. Ancestors be proud of you." He patted her shoulder.

137

Ma. Ma would've been proud of her. Coming West all this way on her own, marrying someone she'd never seen, settling into the ranch. *My ranch*, she thought suddenly. Smiling, Sarah lay back on the bed and passed out.

There was something she had to do. Something that would make a circle of Alex's death, instead of a broken line that trailed off. Sarah turned over and groaned. She licked her lips. They felt like dried pancakes. She reached out and groped around the bed. Empty.

She rose and lit the kerosene lamp. Pulling on Alex's overcoat, she put her nose to the sleeve. It had a comforting cattle smell. From the trunk in the corner, she took Goody's package. She listened; it was quiet outside, the cattle's bawling stopped.

In thick farm boots, Sarah tried to walk silently through the front room. Everyone was gone, the tables cleared. Sarah moaned. Her stomach sloshed and her head ached. She set the lamp on the top step and stood on the earth in front of the house. She'd meant to do this earlier, but hadn't had time. Kneeling, she took up a stick and loosened the dirt. She took out a bulb and looked at it; a thin, green shoot grew from its top. She tucked it at the bottom of the hole, then tamped the earth over it. Ma's scilla. Here, in the Montana earth. Another hole: bury the bulb in the ground. Like Ma, like Alex. She plunged her hands into the dirt and sniffed its good, wet smell. She made a border of holes, zigzagging in front of the house. In each, she pressed the scilla a finger-length in, singing softly, "Bulbs grow, send up green leaves, grow, make pretty flowers, grow, grow," crooning like a child.

138

The lantern flickered across the dirt and Sarah. Then the door opened and a streak of light widened over her.

"Lady? Is that you?" Chang stuck his head out.

"Yes, Chang. I'm planting." Sarah put the last bulb in, patted the earth, and stood.

"You all right?" He stepped down and took her arm.

"Of course, Chang! I *feel* rotten, but that's the whiskey. I had to plant those bulbs. From Ma's garden. Scilla, Chang."

"Of course, lady. Flowers very important." Solemnly, he walked Sarah back and forth, tramping the earth, then helped her up the steps and inside.

He led Sarah to her room, took off the coat and boots, and tucked her into bed. For an instant, she thought Goody stood by her bed, gray braid over one shoulder.

"You're so alike."

"What, lady?"

"You—and Aunt Goody."

"Go to sleep, lady. Tomorrow be better." Chang blew out the light and shut the door. Sarah began to cry, as she realized that Alex would never see Ma's scilla.

CHAPTER SEVENTEEN

"Dear Goody." Sarah pulled her shawl tighter, got up, and fed the cookstove. She tried some coffee left over from yesterday and spat it out. Holding her head, she went back to the kitchen table and sat. Her mouth felt like an uncleaned stall. Outside, a red light shone across the prairie. An owl winged its way home, and a wind followed, rippling the grass. She licked the nib of her pen, winced, and began again.

"Dear Goody, My husband is dead." No, too sudden. Better to start, "Dear Goody, You'll never imagine what happened." No, too light. "Dear Goody"—the pen sputtered—"Things have changed at High Ridge since I last wrote. I wrote you about the snow finally going and how we all became more cheerful. I told you that the spring roundup would happen soon, and how much I wanted to go. I went, Goody, and I wish I hadn't.

"Goody, I feel so sad and I didn't expect it. Alex is dead. He died in a sudden fall, an accident on the roundup. I shouldn't have gone. He said not to, but of course I went. You know I can't bear anyone telling me what to do."

But *was* it her fault? By being there, had she made him more reckless? There was no way she could ever know. Jake said accidents like that happened all the time, even to experienced and seasoned riders.

Sarah sighed and wiped her nose again. She half-expected

to hear Alex's snores, to hear his feet thumping across the floor.

"I don't know what will happen now, Goody. Alex has left me the ranch. I may stay—I may not." Sarah looked out the window and watched the light widen and spread over the prairie. She saw a fox running through the grass, jaws clamped on something. A bird made a sound like a bell. The sky grew purple, then green, and blazed yellow along the horizon. A Maine sky never looked like this. What was there to go home *to?* Silly boys, a father who never talked, and an aunt at the end of her life. And no Fred, no Jake, no William. No Chang, she thought, with surprise. Chang, who brought Alex back; who baked all night to protect the honor of the house. No Sophie, who put her head on your shoulder. No mountains bluer than the Maine sea. She wrote, "Goody, I haven't decided yet, but will write once I know. I miss you and wish you were here, more than you can know. The house is too big and too quiet. Sometimes, I guess you don't know you like a person until they're gone. It's a burden to be so young, but it seems I'll have to grow up at last. Your loving niece, Sarah."

There was a soft knock on the doorjamb, and Chang entered. "How lady feel today? Mmm?"

"Awful. Lady feel terrible. Everything Aunt Goody said about whiskey is true. Devil's brew. Ooh!" She clutched her head. "Why would anyone *want* to drink it, Chang?" The image of a ravaged face with open mouth, snoring, passed swiftly through her mind.

Chang shook his head. "I don't know. Sometimes people sad. Sometimes mad. Then they drink." He shrugged his

141

shoulders. "Lady need tea, with special herbs." He boiled up some water and poured it over a handful of gray leaves in a pot. A bittersweet smell rose.

Chang poured it out for her, making small clucking sounds. "Drink—feel better soon. Special medicine Indians use."

Sarah sipped. It was astringent and made her mouth feel cleaner. She could feel the tea flowing down, settling on top of her roiling stomach. "Ahh. Thank you, Chang. You really are more like my Aunt Goody than you could ever know."

"Mmmph."

"Is Fred up yet?"

Chang looked out the window and nodded.

"Tell him I want to see him in the living room in ten minutes."

"Yes, lady." Chang disappeared, his feet quiet on the floorboards.

Sarah thought how silent he was, how soothing. He never asked, he just *was*. She went into her bedroom and changed into a dark blue riding skirt, blue jacket to match, and pinned her hair firmly into place.

In the living room, Fred stood by the door. He looked somewhat pale, and his lanky hair seemed stringier than ever.

"Morning, missus."

"Good morning, Fred. You may sit down," she said formally. "Chang—would you please bring us some coffee and biscuits? Help repair the damage of yesterday." She smiled.

Fred attempted a grin and failed. "Repair, ma'am? It'll take more than coffee," he burst out. "What's to become of us, eh? Where will we find work? What if the man who buys

142

High Ridge doesn't want *us* and brings in his own hands, eh?"

Is that what would happen if she left? Would Jake and William and Fred, not to mention Chang, all have to leave? She patted her hair and took a tentative nibble on the corn cake, deciding her stomach could take it.

"Well, Fred, don't wear yourself out, now. I don't know *what* I'm going to do yet. I may stay—I may not. So don't plan on leaving just yet."

Fred took a quick look at her, buried his nose in the cup, and commenced sloshing coffee into his mouth. Then he looked up again and said bitterly, "I'm forty years old, ma'am. Not everyone wants a hand that old. They want young 'uns with legs like whippets."

"Mmm." Maybe that was how Alex felt: old in a land of young whippets. And he had had to ride faster and harder and dance longer to make up for it. She sighed and stood up.

"Fred, I need someone to take me around the ranch and explain everything to me. How things work, what goes where, what happens when, all about pastures and grasslands and cattle and"—she paused—"all of that."

Fred stared at her. "A lady rancher?"

"I don't know, Fred." She smiled—lady rancher had a nice ring to it. But what about winters and Indians and those two thousand acres and cattle? Could she do it on her own? What did Alex have in mind when he left the ranch to her? She almost wished he hadn't done it; then she wouldn't have to decide.

Fred scratched his beard. "Well, first thing is to saddle up the horses and we'll go for a ride."

"Can our stomachs take it?" Sarah grinned.

" 'Course. We're not Easterners." He attempted to grin,

143

and that wavering smile warmed her—she was not an East-erner in his eyes, she was a *Westerner.*

He led the way outdoors and called to William to saddle up Sophie and his own horse, a black gelding. William led the horses to them, assuming a mournful expression.

"Stop it, William." Sarah stepped on the mounting block.

"Stop what, ma'am?"

"That false sorrow. I know you're sad about Mr. Proud. So am I. So is Fred. But sad faces are for people with nothing to do. We've got a lot to do." She swung her leg up over the mare and tightened the reins.

"We do?" William looked up at her.

"Yes, you must keep on as if Al—Mr. Proud were still alive. Until I know what my . . . plans are." What plans did she have? Back home to Dewborne? Farther west to Oregon? She supposed she could go anywhere she wanted, but the thought made her button her jacket more tightly, as if a chill wind blew.

Sarah led the way through the gate, and Fred followed. William waved his hat at them and hurried to close the gate.

"What will he be doing today?" she asked.

"Don't rightly know," Fred answered. "Mr. Proud always told us what to do at breakfast. You remember."

"Yes, I remember." Sophie broke into a gentle trot over the grass. A prairie dog poked its head over a mound of dirt, chattered at them, and disappeared. Inexplicably, she felt cheered. "Well, *if* Alex had been at breakfast this morning, what do you think he would have said?"

Fred pushed his hat back with one hand and jogged beside her. He looked at home to Sarah, not an assemblage of un-related parts—shanky arms and dangling wrists, lanky legs, and a head too small for his body. He looked lean and fit and as if he belonged on a horse.

"He'd probably say, 'Fred, you and William work on mending fences. Jake, you go to town and get news and supplies. I'll work in the barn.' "

"He'd say that?"

"Yes'm."

Ahead the land rose slightly, and they jogged up it slowly. Fred reined in his horse, and she stopped beside him. All around was the green prairie, stretching like an ocean to a flat horizon. Cattle grazed in the distance, and birds popped out of the grass and swung on its stems. Overhead, thin clouds blew in a wind of their own. Fred breathed in. "All this is yours." He swept an arm from side to side, "Your land goes up to Mr. Halley's—the English rancher—all the way to the town boundaries. Mr. Proud once told me he had over two thousand acres."

Mine. Sarah put a hand to her chest. She hadn't felt it before, a hunger inside when looking at the land. That the land filled, like cream in the mouth.

" 'Course we've had some trouble with grass pirates."

"Who're they?"

"People who came out later than we did. Tried to set up claims by herding their cattle on the prairie. Pests and rascals, most of 'em."

"Are they going to trouble us?" Sarah patted the mare's neck.

"Ranching's trouble, ma'am. Grass fires, winter, wolves, Indians—anything can happen. But everything you can see here is yours—and then some." He turned and smiled.

Hers. But full of unexpected dangers. And losses. She

145

could lose all the cattle and wind up without a cent. It could happen, and did, to people more experienced than she.

"What else, Fred? What else should I see?"

"Well, you could go back and see how William and Jake are doing on the fences."

"Why would I want to do that? Don't they do what they're told?"

Fred just turned his horse and kicked it to a trot. Sarah followed, up across the prairie, the scent sweet in her mouth. It tasted like bread in the warm sun—earth bread.

In the distance, she saw the fence zigzagging past the barn. There were still some cattle in the corral, left from the roundup—cows that hadn't recovered from the winter.

"Mr. Proud always wanted to give them a chance," Fred said. "He'd try doctoring them up first."

The line of the corral blurred as Sarah remembered her first day here, when Alex brought in the sick ewe from the barn and they nursed it together.

"What would he use?" She wiped her nose hastily. As they rode nearer, Sarah could see Will bending over the fence and Jake standing nearby.

"Blackstrap molasses. Cod liver oil. Sometimes old Indian remedies."

They rode up to the other two and stopped. Jake was not working but smoking, his fingers curled around a hand-rolled butt. He grinned and bowed to Sarah.

"Hello, ma'am."

"Put it out," she said.

"Pardon?" He still grinned.

"I said, put it out! I won't have my men smoking on the

job, or smoking near the grasslands." She watched Jake slowly grind the butt with his heel.

Without another word, Sarah turned the mare and kicked her to a trot. Fred followed close behind, and they came back through the gate to the mounting block. He swung down to help her off, but she said, "No, I'll do it myself, thank you." She slid off the mare, unsaddled her, and gave her a slap. Sophie cantered off to the far side of the corral and began to graze.

Fred glanced at her. "Good start, ma'am—that is, *if* you're staying."

"Mmm." Sarah dusted her hands.

"My ma always said, 'Begin as you mean to go on.' "

Sarah stared out along the fences and wished Alex were still here. She was too small to run a ranch single-handed—too young. "I'll have to grow up at last," she'd written Goody. But *this* way? So quickly, with so many watching?

CHAPTER EIGHTEEN

Sarah watched them ride over the prairie. Three men in black hats, mounted on expensive horses—round, full-fleshed high-steppers. They rode along the gray fences, one of them gesturing at the house and the long, low barn. Another swept his arm wide, from one side of the ranch to the other. Sarah saw his lips move.

And knew. She tightened her belt, smoothed her bloomers and matching jacket, and went into the front room.

"Chang? Put some coffee on. The vultures are here. Only took them two days."

He chuckled and went to make coffee. Soon there was a smart rap on the door. Sarah opened it.

"Mrs. Proud?" A tall man with a red face inclined his head. "May we come in? I'm Mr. Halley, your next-door neighbor. And these are my friends, Mr. Collins and Mr. Wheatley." They nodded and followed the rancher into the room. They stood awkwardly for a moment, eyeing the room and its contents.

Sarah gestured. "Won't you sit down, gentlemen? My cook is making coffee." They bunched their knees under them and perched on chairs near the fire. Though it was June, she kept a fire burning to ward off the morning chill.

Chang brought in coffee and handed around blue mugs. Sarah passed a plate of sugar cookies and stood by the fireplace. "Now, gentlemen, how can I help you?"

148

Mr. Halley cleared his throat. "Well, ma'am, Mrs. Proud, we're wondering—that is, we've been riding around your ranch—"

"I know," she interrupted. "I saw you."

"Yes." He cleared his throat.

His friend Mr. Collins broke in. "Ma'am, we guessed you'd be going back home to your folks, seeing as ranching ain't for ladies, and we came to talk business."

"Yes," the other said, fingering the edge of his dark hat. "Talk business."

Sarah tapped her foot on the hearthstone. *Ladies!* That hated word. Maybe she wasn't one. What had Mountain Jim said? "World don't allow for different kinds of women, gal." Maybe she'd be a new kind—not quite respectable, not quite "loose."

Mr. Halley rattled on, in his high English voice. "I'm sure you have family back East who'll be glad to have you home. You'll be a rich widow, Mrs. Proud." He smiled and nodded.

Sarah tapped her foot and Blitzen growled.

Mr. Collins slurped his coffee and said, "Let's be plain, ma'am."

"You already are." Sarah smiled.

"Ma'am? Let's be plain." He found the end of his thread and went on. "We would like to buy this ranch. We're going into business together and will offer you a good price. It's getting harder and harder to find a spread like this."

Sarah adjusted her bloomers and was gratified to see Mr. Halley eye them disapprovingly.

"Find a spread like this, yes," Mr. Wheatley intoned.

Just like the sewing circle at home, Sarah thought. Drone,

149

drone, bore, bore. She patted Blitzen's head, liking the solid, warm roundness under her hand.

There was an uneasy silence.

"Well, ma'am, what do you say?" asked Mr. Halley. "Can we make you an offer?"

"Why, surely, gentlemen, you can make me an offer." And then and there she decided. "Ranching ain't for ladies," indeed! She'd show them—the vultures with their shiny black hats and red faces.

They leaned forward in their chairs and smiled.

"You can offer your support, your help, your know-how, if you like. Chang?" she called into the kitchen. It was the same feeling she'd had tossing gunpowder into the school stove. "Do we want to sell the ranch?"

"Ma'am!" The Englishman frowned. "You don't ask a Chinese *cook*—"

"*I* do. Chang?"

He came to the door of the room and patted his cloth hat, looking over the heads of their three guests. He cleared his throat and dabbed at his left eye, until the men began to fidget. "The ranch? Sell ranch?"

The men leaned forward even farther.

"No, Mrs. Proud, not good idea. Remember what we say about happiness?"

Sarah grinned at him.

"Enough to eat? Children by back door? Pig in backyard? Land better than gold, gentlemen, better than gold." He turned and went back into the kitchen.

Sarah smiled. "Well, you heard him, we won't be selling the ranch."

Mr. Halley stood hastily. "Mrs. Proud! Taking the advice of a Chinese. You must be mad."

Mr. Collins rose with him. "Mistake, ma'am, a big mistake. You'll be worn out before you're thirty. You've no idea what it takes to run a ranch, no idea."

"Oh, no?" Sarah stopped smiling. "I know a lot about running a ranch, gentlemen. I know about hot tea freezing in its cup—I know how to pluck a frozen chicken—I know all about skating on the kitchen floor—I know about roundups—I know how to bring back a dead husband—I can ride as well as any man—and I'm younger than any one of you!"

She patted Blitzen's head to try and calm down. "Now, if you're finished?" She stuck out her hand and shook each man's hand firmly, and just a second too long. "I hope we'll be friends and good neighbors. Good day to you." She showed them to the door.

Quickly, they mounted their horses, took a last look at Sarah in the doorway, and rode across the grassland.

"Thank you, Chang." Sarah called to him. "You were perfect—just perfect."

"Silly men." Chang wiped his hands on a trouser leg. "They don't know mistress yet—think she droopy flower. Now they know better." He grinned.

"Yes, now they know better." But did she? Good God, what had her quick tongue gotten her into? Sarah went out the door. Fred was working in the barn and she could hear the high, off-key sound of his singing. Blitzen bayed in tune with him. Jake was farther down the land, mending fences, and William was not to be seen.

Sarah pushed open the gate and walked along the path

151

made by her visitors' horses. The grass rustled about her. This time she didn't want to be on a horse, up above the land, looking down. It gave the wrong feeling. She wanted to be here, in the middle of it. The grasses brushed her ankles, and she walked farther across the prairie, out to a small rise.

Was she crazy? What would Goody say when she found out she was staying at High Ridge? What would happen when another hard winter came and she lost a quarter of her cattle or more to the wind and the cold?

Sarah walked faster, up to the top of the rise. She looked over the prairie, back at the ranch. It snugged into the land, gray and weathered. Nothing seemed out of place, nothing unnecessary. It was like her—plain and useful. Someone had to run the ranch. Why *not* her?

She thought of Alex mounted on his gray stallion, riding like a man of twenty and not sixty. No one told you what you'd miss when someone died. It wasn't that she'd loved him. She hadn't, really. But she'd gotten used to him: the faint cattle smell of his skin, his white hair and thick eyebrows, even his snoring. The way he read to her at night. She missed him.

She looked back at the pine tree with the two stones beneath—Alex and Ada. Ada, as quiet and droopy in death as she must have been in life. But Alex? Lie down and be quiet? Never. She chuckled and strode farther out. Someday there would be another stone under that tree. She guessed they'd have to put something different on her gravestone. It would not read DEARLY BELOVED DRUDGE, GONE HOME. It would read MRS. SARAH PROUD, WOMAN RANCHER. It would not tell of her struggles, of the dead cattle, or the days stuck inside while the blizzard scraped the cabin walls. But it would

152

say there was something else besides being a lady or being someone like Calamity Jane.

Sarah looked at the mountains and breathed in. Something rose from them, like the sweet breath of a patient beast. Sarah breathed in again. The land seemed to hold her. She could feel it pressing up under her feet, the sky curving down to meet the plain like an immense bowl. She was in the center, where she was meant to be. The mountains would always be there, the pines always be dark and green. Owls would call from them, and foxes play in the long grass. This was the closest she would get to forever, and it was better than love. Or was a different kind of love.

Sarah turned and walked back to the ranch, swinging her arms.